Pa~~~~ ~~~~~~~

Welcome

Jack Dillon Dublin Tale 1

ISBN-13: 978-1979307246

ISBN-10: 1979307245

Acknowledgments

I would like to thank the following people for their help & support:

Special thanks to Nick, Roy, Julie, Mittie, and Toui for their hard work, cheerful patience and positive feedback. I would like to thank family and friends for their encouragement and unqualified support. Special thanks to Maggie, Jed, Schatz, Pat, Av, Emily and Pat, for not rolling their eyes, at least when I was there. Most of all, to my wife, Teresa, whose belief, support and inspiration has, from day one, never waned.

I can resist everything except temptation.

~Oscar Wilde

Welcome

Jack Dillon Dublin Tale 1

Patrick Emmett

Chapter One

Dillon woke just after six in the morning. He did a quick check with his eyes still closed, trying to remember the latter part of the evening. His mind suddenly jumped forward with the newsflash. He forgot to pack. He slowly opened his eyes and his next thought was related to the leopard print sheets and hint of perfume. The perfume seemed heavy, maybe lilacs in spring, a lot of lilacs. Close by. Where was he and whose bed was he in?

He cautiously rolled over and stared. She probably wasn't too unattractive, even asleep, drooling and giving off a soft, continuous snore. The black eye mask sporting sequined blue eyes and covering half her face made it difficult to tell.

She was blonde, apparently a natural blonde if he remembered correctly. He was trying to recall her name while at the same time appraise her figure. He gradually recalled the shoulder tattoos, the pierced nipples and the blue stone the size of a quarter piercing her navel. He glanced down and his eyes rested on the tattoo about four inches below her navel, a long-stemmed cherry and then in perfect penmanship the words "Jimmy's Playhouse". Unfortunately, his name was Jack. Jack Dillon. US Marshal Jack Dillon.

It started to slowly come through the fog of the previous night as he studied the woman snoring next to him. A few of the guys in the office had thrown a little impromptu going-away party. Nothing too big; after all, he'd be back from Dublin on Sunday night. He remembered his pals had all hurried home to their wives around 8:00. Since he didn't have anyone to hurry home to he sat at the bar for just one more. Now, the end result of that decision was softly snoring next to him. What the hell was her name? Kerri, Karen, Kathy, Kristi, Katie? He was almost positive it was something that started with a K.

"Mmm-mmm," she sort of half-groaned, then seemed to twitch her lips as she reached over and touched him. She ran her tongue back and forth across her teeth and frowned, no doubt tasting the remnants of a half-dozen Brandy Manhattans. In the next moment she groped with her hand, working her way across his chest then suddenly down between his legs, pausing as a puzzled sort of frown crossed her lips. She sat up, ripped her eye mask off and half-screamed, "Who in the hell are you?"

"Umm, Jack Dillon?" he said, not sounding all that sure.

"What are you…? How did you…? Did we?"

"I think so. At least I'm pretty sure. Umm, you were really good. I think." He added that last bit hoping to sort of smooth things over.

It didn't seem to work. She gave a frantic glance at the digital clock on her dresser: 6:27. For the first time he noticed the framed photo of her standing next to a very large man. She was wearing a bikini, a very small bikini, small enough to show at least the top of her cherry tattoo. The guy wore swim trunks, navy blue. He didn't appear all that fat. In fact, upon closer examination he didn't seem to have an ounce of fat on him, anywhere. He had a squared chin, a direct gaze, abs in a definitive six-pack pattern, a massive chest and a muscular arm wrapped around her shoulder. His hands looked to be about the size of ten-pound hams.

"Oh God, he's going to be really pissed off if he finds out," she said. "Don't you dare tell anyone, but you better get the hell out of here. Jimmy will be home in an hour."

"Jimmy? Home?"

"My husband," she said, rolling out of bed. She yanked the pillow out from underneath Dillon's head, tore the leopard-print pillowcase off and dropped it on the floor. She did the same with her pillow then tore off the sheet covering Dillon's knees and tossed it on the floor.

"He's taking the red-eye in from Vegas. They land just after seven. He has to grab a

8

taxi home, but, well, if you know what's good for you, for both of us, you better get the hell out. What'd you say your name was?"

"Umm, Jack," he said, and held out his hand as if they were meeting at a church social function for the first time instead of staring naked at one another after a night of debauchery.

"Kitty," she said, briefly shaking his hand. She quickly gathered up the sheets and pillowcases from the floor, gave a furtive glance around, then called over her shoulder as she hurried out of the room with the bed linens. "You better get dressed. Jimmy had a fight out at the MGM in Vegas two nights ago. He lost, so believe me, he won't be all that happy."

"A fight?" He had just pulled his boxers on and was casting a quick look around for his other sock.

"He's a heavyweight, up-and-coming they say, that is if he can control that awful temper of his. Jimmy DiMucci."

Dillon decided he didn't really need to find his other sock, and pulled his trousers on. His undershirt was on backward, but so what. He pulled his shirt on, figured he could button it in the car. Then thought, God, my car, where is it?

He hurried out of the bedroom, stuffing his feet into his shoes along the way. She was in a small laundry room down the hall. He stopped halfway to the front door and watched as she stuffed the load of bed linens into the washing machine. Somehow along the way she'd managed to slip on a black thong. The lacy design tattooed across her backside seemed to awaken a hazy memory. He'd already forgotten her name, again, and took a wild guess.

"It was nice to meet you, Katie. Maybe we could hook up sometime when…"

"It's Kitty, dumbass, and don't hold your breath. Hey, just to be safe, maybe do a quick look around for a taxi unloading a big guy with two black eyes before you leave the building."

That sounded like traveling music. "Nice meeting you," he said, and hurried out the apartment door.

It was three flights down to street level. The front door looked about a hundred years old and had a large, oval-shaped window of beveled glass. Dillon gave a quick look out the window, glancing up and down the street. Things appeared to be fairly quiet at this hour, so he opened the door, glanced left and right, then hurried down the half-dozen steps. He spotted his car halfway down the street in the middle of the block. The right front tire was resting up on top of the curb.

"Hey," someone screeched.

He half-jumped, glanced around and then looked up to the third floor in the brownstone. Kitty was leaning out of an open window, wearing just her thong and a sneer.

"You forgot your coat, dumb shit," she yelled, and tossed a navy-blue blazer out the window. A car drove down the street and honked, presumably at her hanging out the window. Dillon took a couple of steps and managed to catch his blazer a moment before it fluttered to the ground.

"Don't even think of calling me, ever," she shouted, then slammed the window closed.

Chapter Two

It was only a twenty-minute drive home. He pulled into the underground parking, hurried up to the fourteenth floor and into his unit. He took a quick shower, and remembered he had planned to do laundry last night until plans changed when he met that woman. He threw a couple of changes of underwear and the cleanest shirt he could find into a small suitcase and headed out onto the street to hail a taxi. Trying to get a taxi was another matter altogether and took about twice as long as the actual ride.

"Where to, pal?" the driver said once Dillon finally got a taxi to stop.

"Four hundred Pearl Street."

"Some kind of trouble, is it?" he asked as he pulled away. He stared at Dillon in the rear view mirror.

"For me? No. Actually, it's where I work."

That brought a surprised look to the driver's face, and he remained quiet for the rest of the drive. Dillon paid the fare, got a receipt and gave him a three-dollar tip. The driver looked at the tip, then at Dillon, but didn't comment.

He wheeled his small suitcase into his office, checked his watch, then hurried to the break room for a cup of coffee. He smiled at a couple of the staff working from cubicles in the center of the office, but only one gave a casual nod in reply as he passed. She was blonde-haired, which immediately got him trying to remember what the woman's name was last night. Kate?

"Dillon, all set for your vacation excursion?" Charles Dearborn. "Charlie" to his face, "Deadborn" behind his back. He was on the fast track. Destined for bigger things, but then that would only be natural if you'd never, ever made a mistake in your life. There was no love lost between the two of them.

"Hey, Charlie, how's it going?"

"Wonderful as always," he said, probably not joking. "Coffee?" he asked as he began to fill his mug.

"That's why I'm here."

Charlie topped off his mug, then set the almost empty pot back onto the burner. "Well, what do you know? Looks like you're in charge of a fresh pot," he laughed, took a sip and headed out the door.

Dillon watched him leave the room, thought about giving him the finger, but waited for the expected move. Dearborn quickly glanced back just before he reached the door and stared, expecting to catch him in the act.

"Have a good day," Dillon smiled.

Dearborn looked disappointed, then headed out the door as Dillon gave him the finger. He opened the top of the coffee machine, tossed the paper filter with the grounds into the trash, placed a new filter in, scooped in fresh grounds, added the water and then waited. When a little more than a cup had been brewed, he pulled the pot out and filled his mug. Coffee kept dribbling out of the machine and onto the burner. Sizzling. The puddle made a hissing sound as Dillon replaced the pot on the burner. More coffee overflowed and ran down the front of the machine and onto the counter. He quickly grabbed a paper towel, mopped up the mess, then hurried back to his office.

He spent the rest of the day until mid-afternoon writing reports and filling out forms. At five minutes to three he took a deep breath, walked down the hallway to the door labeled "Assistant Chief Deputy, US Marshal Service." He took another deep breath and entered.

The room was paneled in dark wood with a large desk fifteen feet from the door, and centered perfectly in the room. Behind the desk, sitting ramrod straight behind a spotless desk, sat Meredith Busby, Dahlquist's keeper of the gate. Dillon had always figured she disliked him almost as much as Dahlquist.

Behind Meredith hung a framed painting of the man himself, Dahlquist. He wore a dark suit, with a lean jawline and piercing eyes. He held a rolled up paper of some sort in his hand

14

and his badge was pinned to his suit coat. There was an ongoing auction among staff to buy the painting and use it as a dart board. At just this moment Dillon couldn't recall who had the lead bid.

"Marshal Dillon, here for your three o'clock appointment?"

"Yes," he answered, wondering why the hell else he'd be here.

"The Chief Deputy is on the phone at the moment and you are a few minutes early. Just enough time to perhaps hurry back and get your suit coat," she said, and raised her eyebrows suggesting shouldn't it be obvious.

"Be right back," Dillon said and hurried back out the door.

He pulled his suit coat on over his rolled up sleeves while hurrying back toward Dahlquist's office. He paused outside the door, straightened his tie then entered.

"Oh, so much better. Please, take a seat. I'll inform the Chief Deputy you're here," Meredith said.

Dillon considered reminding Miss Precise that Dahlquist was an *Assistant* Chief Deputy then quickly decided against it.

"Yes, sir, I have Marshal Dillon here for his three o'clock appointment. Yes, sir, he is. Yes. Very well, sir," she said then hung up the phone.

"You may go in, Marshal. You remember procedure?"

"Yeah, knock."

"Excellent."

15

Dillon stepped in front of a pair of wooden doors. The doors had heavy brass knobs decorated with some sort of Victorian design. Each door boasted six inset panels with a beveled edge. He knocked on the door and waited.

"Enter," a voice called from inside, and he turned one of the handles and opened the door.

The room was dark, with wooden Venetian blinds drawn across the four large windows. Two lamps on a carved credenza gave off soft yellow light that drifted over a massive carved wooden desk. There was an area off to the right with a comfortable looking couch and two winged-back chairs arranged around a coffee table. A floor lamp on either end of the couch was turned on and gave off more soft yellow light.

Seated behind the desk was a smaller man with long strands of thin hair combed back over his head. The lights from the lamps reflected off the top of his head and seemed to project the semblance of a halo. The top of the desk was spotless except for a sheaf of papers centered in the middle of the desk and a pen in an elaborate holder positioned at the very front of the desk.

"Be with you in a moment," Dahlquist said without looking up. Dillon stood silently for a few minutes before Dahlquist reached across his desk and took a silver pen from the holder. He groaned slightly as he reached, then seemed to examine something for a moment before he wrote his signature at the bottom, gave a satisfied look and set the pen back in the holder.

"Marshal Dillon, you may take a seat," he said, looking up. No "Thanks for coming." No "How are you?"

Dillon pulled one of three black leather client chairs back and sat down. Not surprisingly, the thing was uncomfortable.

Dahlquist studied him for a moment, then said, "Marshal I'm going to be brutally honest." There was a surprise. "I'm sending you overseas to escort Daniel Ackermann back to the United States because you're the only one I can spare for the time this is going to take. Everyone else is too important and I can't spare them at the moment. You will be accompanied on the flight back by a member of Ireland's Garda Síochána, their police force. I think it goes without saying we do not need an incident of any sort. You will be representing the entire service. I hope I'm making myself clear?"

"Yes, sir, very."

Dahlquist gave a momentary look like he didn't believe him. "Very well then, I'll expect a full report Monday, upon your return."

"Yes, sir."

"Any questions?"

"No, sir. Thank you for the opportunity."

"Hardly an opportunity, Dillon. You're simply the only one I can spare. All right, then. Dismissed."

Dillon stood up from the chair, repositioned it exactly where it had been arranged, then left the office.

"Finished so soon?" Meredith said as he closed one of the double doors behind him, then gave an evil smile.

"Yes. Enjoy the rest of your day," he said and hurried out of the office. He grabbed another cup of coffee, made a couple of phone calls, and cleaned off his desk, then wheeled his suitcase out the door and down to the street. He hailed a taxi and headed out to meet friends.

"Where you off to?" the driver asked, taking in the suitcase.

"Quick trip overseas, back Sunday night."

"That's barely long enough to adjust to the time change."

"Just long enough to have me even more screwed up when I return."

"Ain't that just the way. We go back to Spain every couple years to see the wife's folks. Lovely people, nice place, but I come back here and think, as screwed up as we are, this is still the best show in town."

"Yeah, well I'm headed to Dublin, so we'll see if I feel the same way Sunday night."

"Who you flying?"

"Actually I just need to head down to the lower East side. I've got a meeting there first."

"Busy man," the driver said as he pulled away from the curb.

Chapter Three

"Here's to you, Dildo." Gary Olson smiled, then raised his glass of sparkling mineral water in a toast. Dildo, Dillon's nickname ever since he'd joined the Marshals Service.

"Yeah," Brian Douglass added. "I don't know how in the hell you managed to pull this off, but well done, Dildo." He raised his glass as well and they toasted Dillon.

"To Dildo," the three of them said and clinked glasses. More than a couple heads turned.

They were seated in a corner booth at Spitzer's, a trendy bar on New York's lower east side. They worked together, all three of them US Marshals. The occasion was Dillon's evening flight to Dublin on assignment to escort Mr. Daniel Ackermann back to the US. Ackermann, a fugitive banker wanted on a series of federal charges, had fled the States back in 2012 and disappeared. He surfaced in Ireland in early 2015. Two years of legal wrangling had finally come to an end. He'd been detained in Dublin after attempting to flee to parts unknown using a false passport. Dillon's assignment, compliments of *Assistant* Chief Deputy Dahlquist, was to make sure Ackermann was returned to the States safe and sound. Six hours of watching a movie or reading a book, and a so-so meal. Nothing like having an exciting weekend.

"The thing none of us can seem to figure out, Dildo, is how you managed to snag this gig. Time in Dublin, all expenses paid, compliments of the US Marshals Service. You been over painting Dahlquist's house or working in his garden?How'd this happen?" Olson said.

Dillon smiled, sipped his Coke and wondered if women in Ireland got tattoos like Katie or Kathy or whatever her name was. In truth, no one was more surprised than he was at receiving the assignment. His boss certainly wasn't fond of him. His pals had been chomping at the bit to get the nod for this gig, but somehow it fell on Jack Dillon's desk. He wasn't about to question the fact that Dahlquist said he was the only one who could be spared. A dig at Dillon, yeah, sure, but who cared? He was going to Dublin.

"Don't make it sound like a vacation. I've got to contact the Dublin cops the moment I arrive and turn right around and bring this prick back to serve his sentence. Seven years, I might add, plus whatever they tack on for fleeing. I'll barely have a chance to adjust to the time change over there. Five hours, I might add. I'll have just a moment or two to rest in whatever top notch, exclusive hotel suite they've got me booked into."

"Contact the Dublin cops? Are you kidding? They're meeting you at the airport, probably the second you step off the plane. Christ, they'll probably have someone lined up to carry your suitcase. Contact the Dublin cops, that'll take all of thirty seconds, and then you've got a couple of days left to try and hit every pub in Dublin. Not to mention trying to find some woman stupid enough to spend the night with you."

"I'm missing my mom's birthday, for Christ sake, and, I might add, I'll be working the weekend, giving my all for the service while you two are home relaxing."

"Breaks my heart…not," Douglass said and shook his head.

"Three little girls in dance lessons," Olson said. "Saturday and Sunday at our place is crazy."

"Look, guys, what can I tell you? Old pain in the ass Dahlquist looked at his staff, decided he'd want to avoid an international incident and figured he'd just better send his very best. It's not like it's rocket science. Naturally, that was me and he…."

"Come on, Dahlquist? The bastard hates you. You're usually the first one on the list for every lousy post that comes along. You must have something on him. You got pictures of him and that Meredith?" Olson said.

"Please don't go there. I don't even want to think about that," Douglass said. "Dahlquist hates you? I'd say that's putting it mildly. Then again, don't feel like the Lone Ranger, the man hates all of us."

"Maybe he's had a change of heart. I think he's finally seen the error of his ways, realizes even he can make a mistake once in a great while. Let's just say I'm getting my just reward," Dillon suggested and then thought, not for the first time, it really didn't seem to make sense.

"Dahlquist has a heart? Dahlquist realized he made a mistake? You know, whatever it is you're smoking is against the law. Got any to share?" Olson said, and they all laughed.

"I know, I know. I've been trying to figure it out, too. Then I started thinking, a six-hour flight from JFK to Dublin, with free wine, should give me plenty of time to ponder the complexities of the situation. I've put in a request with the airline to have a beautiful blonde seated next to me." He immediately conjured up a foggy image of the woman he met last night. Her tattoos, the piercings, shaved in the shape of a martini glass. Her name started with a K; if only he could remember it he could…but then just as quickly he remembered the framed photo next to her digital clock. *He's an up and coming heavyweight, if he could just control his temper.* He decided not to go there and maybe best to leave their encounter as a one-night stand.

"I don't believe it," Olson laughed.

"It could happen. Never hurts to ask. Probably some sort of lottery, you know, beautiful women all trying to get a seat next to me."

"Stop it, both of you," Douglass said. "It's that banker you're bringing back, right?"

"Yeah, Ackermann. Daniel Ackermann. He and his Russian partner made off with close to three hundred million. They were named in about a hundred-and-fifty-count indictment. Bank fraud, money laundering, wire fraud, conspiracy, the list goes on and on. The FBI arrested both of them in 2007, and Ackermann was released on a ten-million-dollar bond. Obviously with three hundred million in his pocket a ten-million bond would keep him in line. Jesus, he's a banker, of course he can be trusted. He pled guilty to all counts in 2008 and was sentenced to seven years. They continued his bail at the time of sentencing and he was out on self-surrender for like sixty days, if you can believe it."

"You can't make this shit up," Olson said. "And they wonder why these guys keep trying to pull this shit off. Amazing."

"Yeah. At no surprise, he failed to turn up at Fairton Federal Prison once it was time to begin serving his term, surprise, surprise. God, and I can't take an extra five minutes on a coffee break."

"Gee, and he seemed like such a nice guy," Douglass laughed.

"I guess it was a girlfriend..."

"Imagine that."

"...who turned him in. The reward was something like twenty-five grand."

"Is this the guy who told her they were finished and he was going to go to someplace in the Virgin Islands or South America?"

"Yeah, he cleverly bragged how great it was going to be, then dumps her on his way out the door. I think one phone call later he ends up in custody as he's trying to flee. Classic head up the ass."

"Maybe you can get some inside information or stock tips from him on the flight home," Douglass said. "Guy like that, I'm sure he's got the inside track on a couple of deals."

"You kidding? After hitting every pub in Dublin, not to mention the mob of gorgeous women he'll meet in Dublin over the course of forty-eight hours, Ackermann will have to take care of Dildo."

"Unbelievable."

"Listen, fellas, relax. I'm going to be spending any free time I have visiting churches and saying prayers for everyone in the office. I intend to say a couple of extra prayers for the two of you. You're bound to feel the extra grace of our Lord once I mention you to him."

"I believe half of that. You'll probably end up on your knees, that's for sure, but it won't be due to praying."

"One can only hope," Dillon said and smiled.

"Ahh, Dildo. Couldn't happen to a nicer guy, and just so you know, we're all jealous. You don't think it's too late to put in a request for assistance? I mean me and Douglass, here, we'd be only too happy to help. Guide you on your way, as it were, past all the various temptations."

"You know, I thought about that, got the request approved as a matter of fact, but the Irish embassy denied entry to both of you. So now I've got to just struggle on alone. God only knows, try as I might I'm likely to fall for a temptation or two, but how will I ever know it's the wrong thing to do unless I experience it for myself? Not to worry, I'll pass on any information I come across."

"Maybe just pass on a phone number or two."

"Shut the hell up," Olson laughed.

They chatted for another forty minutes, then grabbed a taxi out to JFK Airport. Olson and Douglass flashed badges at security while Dillon went through with the few thousand passengers waiting in line. They walked him to his boarding gate. Along the way they stopped in the duty-free store, each of them choosing a special bottle of Jameson which they then put on Dillon's credit card. They waited with him at the gate for maybe ten minutes, then said their goodbyes and wished him a safe journey.

Chapter Four

"Ladies and gentlemen, our new departure time will now be twelve-fifteen AM, New York time."

A groan went up from everyone seated in the gate area. It was the third new departure time they'd heard over the course of the last four hours. Kids were crabby, parents were crabbier and no one smiled. Dillon looked at his watch and did some quick math, figuring he'd already lost the better part of a half day in Dublin and he hadn't even boarded the plane yet.

"Bollocks. We should be halfway home by now," a voice from somewhere behind Dillon whined.

"What a bunch of eejits," someone else chimed in.

So this is what international travel is like, Dillon thought. He went back to scanning the crowd for an attractive woman. He spotted more than a few women who fit the bill, a couple of blondes, a redhead and an Asian girl who actually stared back at him for a brief moment. He dared to hope one of them might land in the seat next to him.

The 12:15 departure time came and went. By this time people were stretched out on the floor, sleeping. One young couple on the floor seemed to be linked in an intimate embrace just beyond the last row of chairs. She raised her head for a moment and Dillon realized it was the redhead he'd put on his 'hopeful' list. From what he could tell they appeared to still be clothed.

The waiting seemed to go on and on. A couple who appeared to have been deliberately over-served had been engaged in an argument for the past twenty minutes over his gift of a pasta maker the previous Christmas. By now it was almost two in the morning, and even the babies had stopped crying.

There was a new group of airline staff at the desk next to the boarding door looking thankful that most of the crabby folks had either drifted off to sleep or were comatose. A few minutes later a fresh voice came over the PA system once again.

"Ladies and gentlemen, rise and shine. Flight seven-six-two-eight will begin boarding in just a few minutes. We'd like to invite all our passengers who at this time will need special assistance to approach...." A cheer groaned out from those few still awake in the crowd. Those passengers camped out on the floor slowly stretched and began to sit up, smacking their lips and rubbing their eyes. One or two babies screeched. The couple on the floor behind the last row gave a final few frantic bumps and grinds before he rolled off her and she sat up wearing a smile.

Forty minutes later, Dillon was seated in an aisle seat toward the back of the plane. Seat 38B to be exact. He waited as some guy kept bumping against him while attempting to cram a too-large suitcase into a too-small space directly over Dillon's head. He was about to say something when the flight attendant told the guy he'd have to check the suitcase and the guy grudgingly went back up the aisle, muttering all the way.

The window seat next to Dillon was still empty as the line of boarding passengers began to thin out. At this point he decided he'd be just as happy, in fact maybe even more so, if a gorgeous blonde never showed up. Careful what you wish for.

Chapter Five

She caught his attention the moment she oozed into the cabin and he prayed it wasn't going to happen. She stopped for a second or two and said something to the sexy-looking, blonde, flight attendant. He was too far away to hear what she said, but whatever it was, the words wiped the polite smile off the flight attendant's face and she stood there wide-eyed, apparently speechless and looking shocked.

She was large, very large, make that extremely large. So large that she had to walk down the aisle at an angle, and even then her massive stomach, enormous thighs and jiggling rear bounced off the seats on either side of the aisle. She was clad in possibly the largest florescent pink garment he'd ever seen, billowing cloth draped down to her ankles. Massive forearms, easily the size of his thighs sported a large dimple where her elbow would be. Her hands looked like links of bratwurst.

Her chins seemed to spread out to the ends of her shoulders, eliminating any semblance of a neck.

The suitcase she pulled behind her seemed to crash into every other row of seats, which caused her to sneer at whoever had the misfortune of being seated in her way. As she passed, heads leaned out into the aisle and looked back at the massive body that had just waddled past. A number of people stood and turned round to stare, no doubt eager to learn where she would eventually settle. One woman gave her the finger and looked about to say something until the man she was with put his hand over her mouth and whispered something in her ear.

Oh, God, no, please don't let this happen, Dillon silently pleaded, and then quickly followed up his request with a number of very quick, sincerely heartfelt prayers.

The odds she might take some other seat continued to decrease at an alarming rate with each thundering step she took. Unfortunately, she stopped at row thirty-eight and glared down at Dillon through blue jeweled glass frames as a wave of heavy perfume enveloped him like a cloud of mustard gas.

"I believe we have the window seat," she said, then oozed back a few steps so he could step out of his seat and let her in.

"How about if I give you a hand putting your suitcase up there?" he asked and smiled.

"Please," she said, making the word sound more like a command than a thank-you.

Experience had taught her that in these situations one had to take control. Immediately. She was too large for Dillon to reach past her so she hoisted her suitcase up, careful not to brush against the contraband wedged in her cleavage. In the process she nearly decapitated the individual across the aisle in 38C.

"Hey, watch it," the guy shouted, and picked his baseball cap up from the floor and rubbed his head.

She ignored him, and thrust the suitcase toward Dillon, forcing him back a step or two, then she turned and began the process of wedging herself into the window seat.

Dillon hoisted her suitcase up over his shoulder and crammed it into the overhead bin. He noticed the two guys in the seats behind him had gone red-faced and were silently laughing. The balder of the two had tears running down his face. Dillon just rolled his eyes and shook his head.

She had wedged herself in front of his seat, reached down and raised the arm between the two seats, then forced her way over toward the window, a version of ten pounds in a five-pound bag. Her thighs appeared to be easily twice the size of Dillon's waist. The fluorescent pink garment had wedged up her butt crack, and as she fought her way toward her seat she reached back and extricated the cloth with a meaty thumb and forefinger then dropped into the seat.

The seat gave a loud cracking sound and the two red-faced guys behind her suddenly weren't laughing anymore. The one directly behind her seat automatically thrust both hands up in an effort to stop her from falling back. Not that it would have done any good.

"If you'll excuse me, I think I'll use the restroom before we take off," Dillon said, then hurried toward the rear of the plane in search of a flight attendant to rescue him.

Three of them were huddled together, nervously chatting and shaking their heads as he approached. The attendant facing him directed her attention toward him, and the dark-haired attendant with her back to him suddenly turned round to face him.

"Excuse me, sir, I'm afraid you'll have to take your seat. We're just about to take off." She flashed a pseudo-smile showing teeth which suggested she was dealing with yet another passenger who didn't seem to listen to the safety announcements. Her face took on a look that said at this rate they were never going to get off the ground

"Actually, I was hoping you could put me in another seat. Any seat will work for me."

"Another seat? Does there seem to be a problem? We're almost ready to take off, we'll be departing just as soon as everyone get's seated."

"No, there doesn't *seem* to be a problem. There is a real, major league problem. The woman sitting next to me should have purchased two tickets. She's huge."

"Oh, must be the pink moo-moo dress," she said by way of explanation to the two attendants standing next to her. They nodded in agreement.

"Sorry," one of them said.

"I was just about to bring a seatbelt extension up to her. You're in row thirty-eight, is that right?"

"Yeah."

"I'll bring that extension up in just a moment."

"An extension? We're in seats A and B. Only, she's taken up both seats, there's no room for me. Can't you move me to somewhere else? I'll have to stand for the entire flight."

"I'm afraid we can't do that. I'm sorry, but as you can see it's a completely full flight."

"What about first class?"

"I'm sorry, but that's full as well."

It was at this point that Dillon decided to take command. "Here's the deal, ma'am. I'm a US Marshal, on official business." He pulled his badge out of his pocket and showed it to her, let her have a good long look so she realized who she was dealing with. "Now, I'll be escorting a prisoner back to the States from Dublin this coming Sunday. I have a ticket, it's been paid for, but right now there's nowhere for me to sit."

"I'm sorry, sir. I suppose we could put you on tomorrow evening's flight. That would have you arriving in Dublin the following morning. You'd still be able to make your return flight on

Sunday." The two women behind her nodded like this somehow sounded like an acceptable alternative.

"No, that won't work. I've people meeting me tomorrow morning, paperwork to review with the local authorities. You can't move me up to first class? Or even move her?"

All three of them seemed to look at him for a solution to the problem. "I'd really better get this extension up to her," the flight attendant eventually said, and hurried away.

"You can't help me?" he asked the other two attendants with the blank looks on their faces.

"Like we said, sir, I'm afraid the flight is sold out. There simply are no other seats available."

"What about the cargo hold?"

They smiled and shook their head.

"So I'm screwed?"

"Afraid it looks that way, sir."

He walked dejectedly back up the aisle. "Good luck," the flight attendant who had run off with the seatbelt extension said as she hurried past back toward the rear of the plane. Her tone suggested there wasn't a snowball's chance in hell it was going to work out. A voice suddenly came over the intercom telling everyone to take their seat and that as soon as they were seated the plane would be cleared for takeoff.

As Dillon approached the seat he became aware of a number of air vents on in the immediate area, all loudly blowing air. As he

34

drew closer to his seat the smell of a sickly sweet perfume seemed to hang like a cloud. The arm between their two seats was up and her massive thighs, stretching the fluorescent pink cloth, oozed more than halfway across his seat. He felt a headache begin to start at the back of his skull, stomp its way up into his temples then throb across his forehead as if someone was inside hammering to get out. He attempted to sit down and wedge himself into what remained of his seat.

"I wonder if you wouldn't mind shifting over just a little more," he pleaded as he attempted to squeeze in next to her.

"There's no room. They make these seats so small, it's absolutely criminal," she groaned just as the plane pulled away from the gate.

He could hear the two guys in the row behind him attempting to silently laugh and failing miserably.

Chapter Six

Dillon did some quick calculations and wasn't all that sure the plane would be able to take off with the weight factor in row thirty-eight, but somehow the flight managed to get airborne. Five minutes into the flight his seat partner looked around then thrust a hand deep into her cleavage. She rummaged around, almost elbow-deep for the better part of a minute before she pulled out a small, scruffy, brown dog with large black eyes. The thing wasn't much larger than a double cheeseburger.

The woman gave an angry glance in Dillon's direction, just to ensure he remembered his place. She raised the small dog toward her face, holding him between her two hands while gently turning him from left to right, kissing him a number of times.

"Yes, yes, yes, you are so good."

God, she's going to eat the damn thing, Dillon thought.

She shot another warning glance in Dillon's direction and thought, *You just sit there quietly and don't you dare say a word*. Then she held the tiny animal up and continued to kiss it repeatedly.

"Oh, Mister Nibbles, you are such a good boy. Yes, yes. I know, I know, it's too bad," she cast a quick glance at Dillon from out of the corner of her eye, "but we have to share the seat."

At this point Mr. Nibbles looked toward Dillon and growled, "Grr-err, grr-err, grr-err."

"Now, now, Mr. Nibbles, we're just going to sit quietly for the rest of the flight and relax. We'll be there in a few hours," she said, then seemed to sort of wiggle back and forth, oozing farther into Dillon's seat and forcing him over toward the aisle.

"A beverage, ma'am?" the flight attendant asked a half-hour later.

"I think just a Coke, better make it a diet Coke and maybe three or four bags of pretzels. You wouldn't happen to have any chocolates in your cart, would you?"

"I'm afraid not." The flight attendant smiled.

Dillon thought he could see the wheels turning behind the flight attendant's eyes.

Mr. Nibbles had apparently scurried back down into her cleavage and at this very moment was no doubt wedged and suffocating in some massive roll of fat, never to be seen again. He almost felt sorry for the little thing, but stopped short of attempting to reach for him.

"When will you be serving dinner?" his seat mate asked. She seemed to look hopeful and licked her lips in anticipation.

"Maybe another hour. Once we've distributed the snacks and then picked up we'll be serving."

"Sir?" The attendant smiled and then a horrified look washed over her face as she recognized Dillon. She was the same flight attendant who told him she couldn't help with the seating, suggesting he could take a flight the following evening if he didn't like it That was just before she ran off to deliver the seat belt extension. "Something to drink, sir?"

He glared back. "I'll have a bourbon on the rocks and one of your evaluation forms."

"Umm, I'm afraid that will be ten dollars," she said and seemed to drift back a foot or two in the event he took a swing at her.

He handed her the ten-dollar bill he'd been folding and unfolding for the past thirty minutes, then pulled down his tray. Instead of lowering all the way down, the tray rested on the woman's stomach at about a forty-five degree angle. Her huge stomach was resting on top of her massive thighs, which together blocked any further tray progress. Dillon looked up at the flight attendant and glared again, thinking, *You have got to be kidding me, and I'm paying for all this?* even though he wasn't really paying.

"I'm sorry, but I'm afraid we don't take cash. Credit cards only, sir," she said, and handed back his ten-dollar bill.

"Really?" he said, snatching the ten from her hands. "Better give me a second evaluation form, one won't have enough room."

At this point his seat mate asked, "I wonder if I could trouble you for another bag or two of pretzels? They're so small, barely anything in them."

The attendant quickly handed her two more bags, then looked at Dillon and thought, *Oh, you poor bastard*. She had a change of heart, poured Dillon a bourbon on the rocks and said, "No charge, sir," then decided the best course of action would be to simply flee the scene, and she hurried up the aisle a couple of rows to get away.

Dillon finished his bourbon and ordered another. The moment the second drink was finished he closed his eyes and prayed he could get some sleep. He slept fitfully, suffering through the recurring nightmare of being chained in a small room with the walls slowly closing in on him. But his fervent prayer for sleep must have been answered because when next he woke, the flight attendant was in the process of collecting two empty dinner trays from his seat mate. She handed both trays to Dillon, then quickly reached up and grabbed an uneaten package of cookies from the top tray.

A moment later the overhead announcement came across, instructing everyone to return their seats back to the upright position. Dillon's stomach gave a loud growl just as his seat mate quickly stuffed the two cookies into her mouth and chewed vigorously.

He rubbed the sleep from his eyes and anxiously glanced over to look out the window as the plane made its final approach over the Irish coastline heading into Dublin airport. It would be his first real view of Ireland. Unfortunately, and not at all surprisingly, his seat mate was completely blocking the window.

The moment the plane came to a stop and the "fasten seatbelt" sign went off, Dillon was the first person bounding out of his seat. The entire left side of his body felt numb. Mr. Nibbles popped his head out from the valley of cleavage for a brief moment, gave a quick growl in Dillon's direction, then ducked back down like the little sewer rat he was and disappeared.

Once off the plane he walked down a large, long corridor with black and white posters of famous Irish individuals hanging from the wall. Sports figures, actors, writers, and musicians stared back at him in earnest as he hurried past. He wove in and out of the crowd of slower-moving passengers heading toward passport control, hoping to get toward the front of the line. The mob of passengers thinned ever so slightly every time it passed a restroom.

He needn't have bothered hurrying, the line for non-EU passports wove back and forth through a mile or two of lanes defined by blue nylon belts. Most of the people standing in line ahead of him had carry-on luggage large enough to hide a body in.

Whoever was at the front of the line had to stand and wait until they were called by one of the passport control officers. There were a good two hundred people ahead of Dillon, another hundred or so filling in behind him, and things didn't seem to be moving all that quickly. As a matter of fact, they didn't seem to be moving at all.

He was in the process of stretching and turning left and right at the waist in an effort to massage a semblance of life back into the left half of his body. After having a couple hundred pounds of dead weight plus Mr. Nibbles draped over it for the past six-plus hours, he could barely feel a thing.

"Mr. Jack Dillon, please. Is there a Jack Dillon here?" a female voice called out from the front of the line.

Thank God, Dillon thought and called, "Over here." He waved his hand above his head. As if in response, a good two hundred heads turned in unison and stared at him.

"One moment, please," a woman called, then walked along the far side of the line toward the lane where he stood. He noticed she was wearing a uniform. She stopped and unhooked one of the nylon belts forming the aisles. "If you'll come this way, please," she said, and indicated he move toward her with a wave of her arm.

"I wonder what that guy's got that's so special?" someone growled from further back in line.

Dillon wound his way past people seemingly still half-asleep on their feet. He edged his way past an exhausted young couple holding two sleeping toddlers, and a group of four college girls carrying backpacks, who looked like they were going to be camping in the wilderness for a month. He wiggled around a business guy in a blue suit coat who appeared to be reading a newspaper and moved over no more than a half-inch so Dillon could just barely squeeze past him.

"Is he the only one?" some guy called as Dillon edged around the foot locker that apparently served as the business suit's carry-on luggage. He stepped past the nylon belts, then waited for the woman to reattach the belt.

"We've all had a very long flight," a woman with a pink suitcase emblazoned with white cat paws said. She had a matching handbag slung over her left arm. A strand of red yarn was tied around the handle of her suitcase, apparently to make her suitcase standout, as if there'd be a number of similar pieces of luggage in any baggage claim area.

So long, my fellow travelers, Dillon thought, not one bit sorry to leave them all standing in line.

Chapter Seven

The woman who had called his name was an attractive redhead, hair just a little shorter than shoulder-length, made all the more attractive by her green eyes and freckles.

Dillon thought, *If this is what they look like over here it's going to make the last six hours worth the trouble.* She wore dark blue trousers, a light blue shirt with dark blue epaulets and a dark blue tie. She sported fairly large breasts, a slim waist, wonderfully curved hips the trousers failed to hide and a smile that would melt you on the spot.

"US Marshal Jack Dillon?" she asked as he stepped forward.

"That's me."

"Welcome to Ireland, Marshal. I'm Garda Ann Dumphy. This way, sir, if you please, and we'll get you out of this line. A long flight, I hear, you're almost five hours late." She indicated a long hallway with her hand, smiled gleaming white teeth and thought, *For being five hours late and six hours behind the local time, you're not too bad-looking. How unfortunate this has to be about business.*

"After you," Dillon said, then followed as she walked him past the passport control stations, down a long hall and toward a door marked "PRIVATE." Her uniform, which appeared to be designed to hide her figure, was fortunately failing at the task, and he continued to admire the enticing view from behind. She opened the door then stepped to the side, holding the door for him to enter the room.

The windowless room they entered had a number of color monitors along one wall. Uniformed Garda were seated in front of every two monitors. Bits of casual conversation occasionally flowed back and forth between the officers. A ceramic mug seemed to be in front of just about everyone.

"How did they even let her on the flight?" someone said.

"God, will you look at that," another replied.

"Better bring her in for a full body search," someone said, and a number of people laughed.

"It'll take days. God only knows what you'll find," another replied, which brought more laughter from everyone.

"She's one for you, Brady. But you'd have to take tops."

Dillon looked over at one of the monitors. Surprise, surprise, his seat mate in the pink moo-moo was taking up the entire screen and then some. Other passengers waiting in line behind her were staring. You could see a couple of them whispering a comment which would then bring a smile to the recipient's face.

God, you think that's bad, you ought to try sitting next to it for six hours, Dillon thought.

"God bless. But would you look at that. Unbelievable," someone said, and a silence seemed to fall over the room as her massive figure drifted into position at the back of the line. She wiggled and squirmed for a few moments, no doubt getting Mr. Nibbles' position adjusted.

"She's smuggling a dog in," Dillon said to no one in particular.

One of the guys in front of a monitor spun round in his desk chair and studied Dillon for a long moment. He wore a blue uniform shirt just like Ann Dumphy's, though nowhere near as interesting. He grabbed a white mug with a Dublin Airport logo in his right hand, took a long, slurpy sip, then pushed his glasses back up on his nose and said, "What was that? You know her? What was she smuggling?"

"I said she's got a dog. She has the thing hidden somewhere in that gigantic pink outfit. I had to sit next to her on the flight. Christ almighty, the left side of my body will be numb for the remainder of the day. Honest to God, she took up two seats and she had this small, little brown dog hidden in her cleavage. The damn thing growled at me."

"Are you serious?"

45

"Absolutely. I feel duty bound to turn her in. She calls the damn thing 'Mr. Nibbles.'"

"Her boobs?" someone called out, and the comment brought laughter from the group.

"No, the wretched little dog. She called him Mr. Nibbles and fed him pretzels during the flight. He's a little brown furry thing, not much bigger than a double cheeseburger. And the damn thing is mean. Like I said, he growled at me. More than once."

"I'm not sure we've a holding room big enough for her," the guy with the mug said, then picked up a phone, pressed a button and began to speak a moment or two later. "Yeah, Kevin, give a look to the far back of the line. There's a very large woman in an absolute tent of a pink dress standing back there. Yeah, I know, impossible to miss."

"They call it a moo-moo," Dillon said.

"Bloody tent is what it is," someone replied.

"Moo, moo," someone called, sounding like a cow, and the room erupted in laughter.

The guy on the phone shot a quick look over his shoulder at the monitor, then spun his chair round to face it and said, "No thanks, I've a bad back. When she gets to the front of the line, pull her out and put her in interview room A. What? No, we've reason to believe she's smuggling a dog in. No, she's actually got it inside the pink outfit somewhere. Yes. Absolutely, a dog rescue, no doubt the thing is about to suffocate."

That last line brought more chuckles from the group.

"Poor thing will be scarred for life," someone said.

Once he hung up the phone he spun back round in his chair. "So you're the Yank? A US Marshal, we hear."

"Yeah, that's right."

"Dillon, is it?"

"That's right."

The accent was very different from the woman who had escorted him into the room, and Dillon had to concentrate to understand it. The man took a sip from his mug and smiled.

"You disappoint me, Marshal. I was hoping for someone in a cowboy hat and boots. And your mates call you Dildo? Is that right?" he said, then looked left and right as everyone had a laugh. The redhead standing next to Dillon glanced at the floor and seemed to chuckle.

"Who told you that?"

"We have our sources. All anonymous, of course."

Dillon kept a straight face and silently cursed Olson and Douglass or whichever former friend it was who gave his nickname away.

"I'm here to escort an American citizen by the name of Daniel Ackermann back to the States. We've got room and board for at least the next seven years just waiting for him, and his appearance back in the US, compliments of the government, is long overdue."

"Another banker. He sounds like a wonderful guy, and you're certainly welcome to him. Officer Ann Dumphy will take you to him. Humphy Dumphy, we call her." A couple of guys laughed, but not everyone, and not Ann Dumphy, whose green eyes, once she looked up from the floor, had suddenly grown very cold.

"So, apparently everyone here has a nickname," Dillon said. "What's yours then?"

"Plonker," someone called from behind, and that brought more laughter from the group.

"Dumphy will get you settled into your hotel accommodations. We've reserved a room at the Gresham for you. Have you been here before?"

"No, first time in Dublin."

The guy turned toward Dumphy and asked, "You've got the packet of contact information he'll need?"

She nodded. "All set, usual signatures needed, but no problems thus far and I don't expect any."

"And Marshal, you brought your paperwork, I trust," he said to Dillon.

"All filled out according to your regulations," Dillon replied and patted his computer bag. "Do you need to take a look?"

"No, thankfully. Just want to make sure you don't have a problem going in. Last minute is not the way to do this."

"I'm with you there."

"Might as well head to the Gresham," he said to Dumphy. "With this flight delay and late arrival you've a bit tighter than normal schedule."

"Yes, sir. I'll bring him there, get checked in and settled, then over to the 'Joy' at three." She glanced at her watch. "It'll be a bit of a tight timeframe, but nothing we can't handle," she said.

"Maybe once you check into your room, you can get cleaned up. With that late arrival you don't have much time before your initial meeting at Mountjoy prison. As long as your paperwork is in order, everything should go smoothly. We'd like nothing better than to get the cost of keeping this knacker off our books."

Dillon nodded, thinking, *Not so fast*, then said, "I don't believe I caught your name."

"Daly," he said, standing from his chair. "Patrick Daly. My friends call me Paddy. It's nice to meet you, Marshal. Listen, not to hurry you off, but it would be bad form to be late. With your initial appointment at three this afternoon, you've barely enough time to grab a shower and change. Everything goes well this afternoon and you'll be at the Four Courts tomorrow morning. What time is that?" he said, and looked at Dumphy.

"The hearing's at ten," she said, then faced Dillon. "It's all rather perfunctory at that point, that is, provided your paperwork is in order. Basically just a rubber stamp."

"There you go, Marshal Dillon. A pleasure meeting you, and thanks for the dog smuggler tip. Now, you enjoy the rest of your day and welcome to Ireland," Daly said, then settled back into his chair, spun round and studied the computer screens in front of him. "Now where is she, your woman in the pink woof-woof with the dog?"

"It's a moo-moo," someone called farther down the line, and everyone chuckled.

"Yes, quite, a moo-moo," he said, sounding like a cow. "God only knows what else she's hiding."

"This way, Marshal. We'll taxi into the city center. Do you have any luggage to claim?" Ann Dumphy asked as she directed Dillon toward the door.

There was a part of him, perhaps a vicious part, that half-wanted to stay and watch the dog-smuggling interrogation of his seat mate, but apparently they were pressed for time.

Garda Dumphy led him through the airport baggage claim area, out a door, down a large escalator and then outside to wait in the queue for a taxi. The line was long, but moving pretty fast. They didn't have to wait more than five minutes before a taxi pulled up and they climbed in.

It was Dillon's first experience with the steering on the right hand side of the vehicle, and he stared from the comfort of the back seat for a long moment. Not bad, he thought. Exotic international travel, as long as you ruled out his seat mate on the flight over. A gorgeous redhead to escort him through the process and maybe even around town if he could talk her into it later on. He could get used to this life.

Traffic seemed to be just like the States, heavy and not making any real progress. The

50

cars were different, not just the right side steering, but the size as well, smaller and more compact. Once they left the actual airport area traffic seemed to move much better. They pulled onto whatever the Irish called their interstate system and picked up speed. Two exits later they pulled onto a city street, and things seemed to move slower.

"You said you'd never been here before?" Ann said.

"No, never to Ireland."

"I hope you like it," she said, then settled back and gazed out the window. Dillon sat back and did the same, looking at the buildings and the people walking down the street. There seemed to be a lot more foot traffic than he was used to, and a number of bicycles. They were headed toward the center of the city, although the area still appeared highly residential with lots of two and three-story buildings that looked to be a hundred years old.

Chapter Eight

It was just after two by the time the taxi dropped them off in front of the Gresham Hotel on O'Connell Street in Dublin's city center. The hotel was just across the street and about a block from the GPO, the General Post Office. It was one of the many historical structures that were shelled in the 1916 Easter Rebellion, back when O'Connell Street was called Sackville Street. Dillon knew this because he'd spent a few nights earlier in the week trying to get a feel for the city while looking at Google images.

Ann Dumphy's voice brought him back to the here and now. "I'll grab a tea inside and wait for you down here so you can get cleaned up," she said as she climbed out of the back seat of the taxi.

Dillon slid across the seat, enjoying the view as she climbed out.

"We're just going over to the 'Joy' to meet with staff. We'll get some preliminary paperwork signed this afternoon. As long as everything is in order you won't have a problem. Come on, let's get you checked in and you can get cleaned up."

"The 'Joy', that's what you call Mountjoy, the prison? That's where Ackermann is being held, right?"

"Yes. The way we work it is, you meet staff this afternoon, they'll do a quick check, make sure everything is in order. Then, tomorrow morning we go over to the Four Courts and appear in front of the magistrate at ten. Once we clear that hurdle you can meet with Mr. Ackermann, if you wish. We'll provide you with security to the airport on Sunday. The two of you will board the plane before anyone else, and then you're off to the States. One of our people will be accompanying you on the flight back over to the States."

"Any idea who that might be?"

"No, I don't. For simple security reasons, they never really let us know in advance."

"Would it be you?"

She smiled then said, "Definitely not." Then seemed to think for a moment and said, "Oh, sorry. I didn't mean that as a reflection on you. It's just that I'm not cleared for that duty."

Dillon smiled and nodded, then said, "I've read Ackermann's file, and I've got an 8x10 black and white photo of him, but I've never met the man. Have you met him? Ackermann? I'm sort of curious to find out what he's like, what he's been up to these past seven or eight years. On the other hand, sitting next to him on the flight for six hours, all that information might at least be something to talk about."

"I've not had the pleasure of meeting him," she said in a tone meaning anything but pleasure. "I'm part of the escort team, but at best I'll only ever see him from a distance I'd guess." She glanced at her watch. "We should probably let you get cleaned up. It would be bad form to be late for your first meeting. We're not that far away."

"I wouldn't dream of being late, Officer...."

"Oh please, call me Ann. I'm to mind you for the next few days, so let's both relax and we'll get on just fine."

"See you shortly," Dillon said, and headed off toward the front desk.

She watched him leave and made her subtle appraisal. *Not bad*, she thought, *and he seems nice.*

She waited for Dillon in the lobby while he hurried up to his room. He laid his clothes out on the bed, shaved, showered and changed. He was back down in the lobby thirty minutes later, tired, but able to get on with it at least for another hour or two now that he'd had a hot shower.

He took the time to notice she'd applied some fresh makeup, and there was just the slightest hint of a nice perfume in the air. Not that she needed any of it. She was the sort of woman who was naturally beautiful, with or without makeup or perfume.

"Oh, all ready to go? Perfect timing," she said, setting a teacup back on the white saucer. She smiled as she stood and absently tugged along the sides of her shirt before they headed for the door. "We'd best take a taxi, Mountjoy is just a few minutes away. Come on."

Dillon followed her out the door and across the street to where a queue of taxis waited. She walked toward the head of the queue where two drivers in shirt sleeves stood talking.

They turned as one and watched her approach, one half-whispering something to the other, who simply nodded. Dillon couldn't hear what was said, but he thought he probably knew the gist of the comment, meant to be a compliment although probably fairly crude. Then the one who whispered the comment stepped forward.

"Right, Officer, now where are we off to?" he said, pulling open the rear passenger door.

"Mountjoy, for the two of us," she replied, sliding into the back seat.

The taxi driver gave Dillon a close appraisal, seemed to double check him, possibly looking for handcuffs on his wrists as he walked to the far side of the taxi and opened the passenger door.

"So the Joy it is then," the driver said once he'd slid behind the wheel and stared at the two of them in his rearview mirror. He seemed to wait a long moment, hoping for some further response, God forbid an explanation. When it didn't come he eventually started the car and drove off in the general direction of Mountjoy Prison.

"Right," Ann said, and didn't say anything further.

The taxi man glanced back at Dillon a few times en route, thinking, *He doesn't look like the criminal type, but then again they're exactly the ones you have to watch.*

"Now, they're going to go through all your paperwork. Don't take it personal, they're really just checking to see if there are any potential problems. If they spot anything, you've a chance to get it taken care of before tomorrow." She glanced at her watch. "It's not even 10:00 back in New York, so you'd have the better part of the day to get whatever you need and we can print if off at our office, or even at the Joy if they'll let us. On any given week we might have three or four transfers like this, although usually it's with another EU country."

"I'm not too worried. Our boss enjoys cracking the whip, so I'm sure everything is in order."

Chapter Nine

"This close enough?" the taxi man asked no more than five minutes later. He'd pulled up in front of a massive stone edifice two stories high with a heavy timbered blue gate centered in the tall, grey stone walls. The place looked to Dillon like the gate to some sort of castle-like fortress, which actually wasn't all that far from the mark. A rounded window was set up high in the thick stone wall on either side of the gate, and below that was a long, narrow window with steel bars painted white.

Ann sat in the back of the taxi for a moment and sent some sort of text message on her phone, then paid the ten-euro fare and asked for a receipt. As they stepped out of the taxi, Dillon looked up at the massive walls and just stared.

"Not the most welcoming structure in Dublin," she chuckled.

"It looks more than a little imposing."

"That was the idea, bit of a gentle reminder to the population at the time. Built by the English around the 1850s, it was originally designed to house people who were to be deported. The English were…" she paused for a moment. "Let's just say, 'very efficient' at their task."

"It gave us Australia," Dillon joked.

"Along with some other things."

Suddenly a smaller door set in the large timber gate opened, and two smiling uniformed guards stepped out.

"You can never seem to get enough of this place, Ann. Always coming back for more. It must be my charming personality," one of the guards said. He was big, heavy in a sort of farm labor way, and bald, with a very pink head. He had a natural smile and sparkling blue eyes.

His partner was tall, lean, and maybe fifteen years younger with dark, close-cropped hair, brown eyes and a prominent nose. His Adam's apple bobbed up and down on his thin neck like a basketball. He didn't seem to respond to the charming personality comment.

"I'm always amazed you're still working, Brian, you know, as opposed to simply being locked up. I just like to stop in and check on you from time to time, see if your status has changed from staff to resident," Ann said. "This is US Marshal Jack Dillon. He's going to be escorting one of your guests back to the States on Sunday."

58

The large guard with the pink, bald head smiled and nodded. "Nice to meet you, Marshal. Dildo, is it?" he asked then flashed a quick, knowing smile and extended his hand.

It had to be one of those two idiots Olson or Douglass, Dillon thought. Passing his nickname on - the two of them deserved a special place in hell for the effort. Once he got back to the States he'd have to come up with something special for both of them.

"I see my colleagues have been in touch."

"Oh, they got us up on all the trash about you. Come on, let's run you through security and get things moving. This afternoon they've got you in conference room C, Ann. Fortunately, for a change, the man in charge seems to be in a semblance of good humor."

"That can't last for long," she replied, and they stepped through the door, walked about ten feet, then stood in front of another entrance, this one adorned with heavy cast iron bars painted a royal blue. Their two escorts each flashed a security badge in front of a scanner, then stood back and waited a good ten seconds before there was a loud buzz and the lock on the cell-like door snapped open. As they pushed the heavy door open it squeaked and groaned on its hinges.

"Bit of a security check, and then we'll escort you to the conference room," Brian the guard said as they walked down a short hallway and into a large room with a massive metal detector and a bored-looking guard. The guard stood from behind his desk and gave a slight sigh at the interruption. Dillon placed his computer bag on a counter, then waited while the unsmiling man searched it, removing the contents one by one, examining them and placing them in a grey-plastic tray. He ran the empty computer bag and the tray of contents through the x-ray machine, then set them back on the counter.

"Turn the computer on so I can determine that it works," the guard said in a monotone, sounding like he'd already given the instruction a few thousand times that day. Dillon turned the computer on. The moment it made the sound indicating it was starting the guard said, "Thank you. Now turn it off, please. I'll need a photo ID."

Dillon handed him his passport along with his Marshal's ID. The guard actually studied the ID for a long moment, looking from the photo to Dillon and back again.

"I know, the picture looks like I should be arrested for war crimes," Dillon joked.

Apparently the guard didn't quite see the humor in the comment, and studied the ID for a little longer. "Please read this form, sign at the bottom stating you're in agreement, then return your computer to its case."

Dillon scratched his signature across the bottom of the form without reading it, and handed it back to the guard.

"You didn't read it," the guard said.

"If I don't sign it you're not going to let me in, right?"

"I can't let you in if you don't sign, it's against the rules."

"There you go."

"This way if you please, Marshal," Brian the guard said, and Dillon followed him through a maze of halls.

"That guy back there must have had a long night. Not the most cheerful person I've met in Dublin."

"Good thing you caught him on one of his better days," Brian said. He didn't appear to be joking. He led them into a conference room with a heavy wooden table that seated eight. The room had three windows with rounded tops looking out onto a small garden plot. What looked like two rose bushes and maybe a half-dozen tomato plants inhabited the garden. The room was empty at the moment, but there were a number of stacks of official-looking documents lined up at one end of the table and a tablet of lined paper with a pen rested in front of four of the chairs.

"You'll sit here," Ann said, and pointed at one of the chairs positioned at the end of the table. "They'll be here in a couple of minutes. Would you like a tea?"

"No thanks," Dillon said just as the door opened and a heavyset guy with shirtsleeves rolled up over massive forearms strolled into the room.

He gave a quick glance around and zeroed in on Ann. "Garda Dumphy, how're you keeping?" he said, nodding, then extended a hand toward Dillon. "And you're US Marshal Jack Dillon, I presume."

"That's right. Nice to meet you," Dillon said, drawing out the last word, in effect asking the question without actually asking.

"Dougherty, Shane Dougherty. Shall we get started? Just some basic things prior to your appearance tomorrow before the magistrate. Are you at all familiar with the prisoner, Mr. Ackermann?"

"Only what I've read. I've never actually met the man. He disappeared from the States once he was due to surrender and begin serving his sentence. I've studied his photo, read up on the charges he was convicted of."

Dougherty nodded in a way that suggested he was familiar with Ackermann's history. "Based on our experience, your transport should go fairly smooth. Nothing even remotely associated with any incidents during his three-month stay here. A model resident, you might say. I can only hope you're in for a very boring return journey."

"I hope that's the case," Dillon said.

"Well then, let's get started. Please, have a seat." Dougherty pulled out a chair, sat down and opened a file. "We'll need you here on Sunday morning no later than...."

It took an hour and twenty minutes from start to finish, and then they were back outside the gate at Mountjoy, waiting for another taxi.

"So," Ann said. "We've the magistrate tomorrow morning at ten. Fancy a quick tour of the area, or maybe you'd rather just go back to the Gresham and close your eyes?"

"Actually, please don't take it personal, but back to the hotel sounds the better choice; I can feel myself beginning to fade. If I tell the taxi man the Four Courts tomorrow will he know what I'm talking about?"

"Oh, yes. But why don't I plan on meeting you in the hotel lobby, say half-nine, and we'll head over together."

"Half-nine?"

"What you'd call nine-thirty."

"I can do that," Dillon said just as the taxi pulled up.

"Come on, let's get you back to the Gresham before you fall asleep on your feet."

"I look that bad?"

"You look...tired."

She dropped him off at the Gresham a few minutes later. He made his way up to his room, kicked off his shoes, took off his coat, draped his trousers over the chair and fell sound asleep face down in the bed about five seconds later.

Chapter Ten

Dillon found himself in the hotel dining room just a little after seven the following morning, this after having had a series of nightmares starring Mr. Nibbles and a pink moo-moo until he was wide awake at four AM. He was there at seven only because the restaurant didn't open any earlier. In a dining room that sat at least sixty, he was the only one seated, and he perused the menu in peace once his coffee arrived.

He ordered what was referred to as a full Irish breakfast: eggs, toast, rashers (bacon), sausages (referred to as black and white pudding) and baked beans. The breakfast was okay, although the black and white pudding didn't impress him all that much. He decided that the puddings, black and white, were just that and indeed not sausages. He made a mental note to stay clear of them for the remainder of his stay, thinking they reminded him more of bird suet and deciding they must be an acquired taste he had no intention of acquiring. If he was honest with himself, he hadn't eaten baked beans for breakfast since a Boy Scout camping trip at least twenty years earlier. Still, all in all, a tasty breakfast, and the coffee worked to get him on track time-wise.

He returned to his room, grabbed a shower, shaved and spotted Ann Dumphy talking on a cell phone and sipping from a white porcelain mug in the hotel lobby at just a little after nine. Based on the crowd, or lack of one, it was still fairly early by local time. By the time he saw her, he was just close enough to hear her say, "Oh, goodness, he's already here. I'll have to chat with you later." She disconnected her phone, set it on the table next to her porcelain mug and flashed a becoming smile.

"Is that coffee?" he asked.

"I wouldn't dream of it," she scoffed, then signaled a server with a wave of her hand.

"Yes?"

"I think we should get a coffee for this gentleman. Anything else you'd like?" she asked and raised an eyebrow.

Appraising her seated there, hair pulled back, just the right bit of makeup, lipstick and the eyes that seemed to flash he immediately thought of the stupid guy line, *I'd like something else, but I don't think they have it on the menu*. Instead he responded with, "No, thanks. I had the full Irish breakfast a little earlier this morning."

"I'll get that coffee for you right away," the server said. She picked up an empty plate from the table and hurried off toward the kitchen.

"Thanks. You didn't have to do that. I...."

"We're about to head into a hearing that will drone on for at least an hour. It wouldn't do to have you falling asleep, bad form. You've your paperwork and files?"

He tapped his computer bag. "Everything's right here. I've got an emergency number at the embassy I can call if I need to. They're supposed to have someone there to do the talking. I just have to show up, smile and pretend to be polite."

"What do you know about the American gentleman you're escorting back to the States?"

"Daniel Ackermann? Like I said yesterday, he is, or rather was, a banker. He and some Russian partner came up with some sort of scheme where they scammed over three hundred million..."

"Say no more. At least in the States you're prosecuting your bankers. Over here they just get away with a wink and a nod and then somehow they all end up on NAMA's payroll. Next thing you know we all suddenly seem to be paying them for misbehaving. It's positively corrupt, and the government makes the working taxpayers pay the bill."

"We've got a fair share of our own investors and Wall Street fat cats who seem to be above the law, or at least act like they are. It will be a pleasure to haul this guy back, one of those situations where you ask yourself how it could ever happen. I can't seem to get away with an overdue book at the library, and these guys...."

"Oh, here's that coffee. Thank you so much," she said as the waitress set a steaming mug on the table.

"Will there be anything else, ma'am?"

"No thank you. We'll finish this and be on our way."

"What do I owe you?" Dillon asked.

"Taken care of," Ann replied, then nodded and the woman left.

He took a sip and hoped he didn't grimace. God, instant coffee, not good. He didn't say anything and forced it down. Twenty minutes later they were in a taxi heading for the Four Courts building.

"You've appeared in front of a judge before?" Ann asked.

"Many times."

"It will be interesting to see if you find the experience in the Four Courts any different."

"Maybe just the costumes and the wigs your guys wear. Like I said, someone from the embassy is supposed to be here and do most of the talking. Guy named Dawson. Ever hear of him?"

"No, umm, I'm afraid not," she said. He was looking out the window at the people and the buildings they were passing and didn't react. But the tone of her response just didn't sound right. He looked at her from out of the corner of his eye, caught her biting her lower lip, and wondered if there just might be some history there. Be interesting to see once they met this Dawson guy. Nice-looking lady like Ann, anything could be possible.

"I phoned him earlier, but never got an answer so I left a message. I just hope he's there."

"I'm sure he will be, they're usually very prompt."

"And you said you never met him?"

"That's right."

"Mmm-mmm, okay," Dillon said, now absolutely sure there was some sort of past history.

Ann just nodded, but didn't bother to reply.

Chapter Eleven

He was there, a man Dillon pegged at somewhere just over thirty, a good-looking guy in a navy-blue pinstripe suit. He was pacing back and forth in front of the courtroom doors, constantly checking his watch about every three or four steps. He carried a worn, leather computer bag under his left arm, embroidered with the maroon and gold seal of Boston College on the flap. Dillon figured he was probably the youngest member on staff and that's why he drew the short straw for this procedure.

"Thomas Dawson?" Dillon asked from behind.

"Yes," Dawson said as he half-jumped, then spun round with a surprised look on his face.

"US Marshal Jack Dillon. Pleased to meet you," Dillon said and extended his hand.

"Oh, man, I didn't know if you'd make it or not. I knew you had some flight problems coming over. You've got the documents?" Dawson asked in a midwest accent.

Dillon placed the accent as maybe western Iowa or Nebraska. "Right here," he responded and patted his computer bag. "All the original paperwork, everything signed and stamped." He noticed Dawson's brief nod toward Ann, made another mental note, this time confirming there was definitely some history there.

"Thank God. I've got copies, but depending on who's presiding they can be a bit particular and might want to see the originals. We don't need anything screwing this up."

"We're covered either way," Dillon said, then watched for a reaction to his next line. "Oh, forgive me, let me introduce Garda Ann Dumphy, my minder during my stay here in Ireland."

"Oh yeah, we may have met once or twice before. Nice to see you again, Officer Dumphy," Dawson replied. He flashed a very quick smile, although his eyes remained cold.

She nodded, flashed a quick smile back, but didn't say anything else. Maybe she looked just a little bit uncomfortable, Dillon couldn't be sure. Neither one extended a hand and there was definitely the hint of some tension in the air. *Interesting*.

"Shall we go inside? We can get up to speed at the conference table. Glad to see you made it. Like I said, I had word of your flight delay waiting for me when I arrived in the office yesterday. Hope you were able to get some sleep. Come on this way," Dawson said, suddenly spewing a continual patter, not really waiting for any response, and turning his back on Ann. He pushed open the giant oak door to the courtroom, and led Dillon inside. Ann followed behind at a discreet distance.

During the entire proceeding Dillon answered just two questions. He stated his name for the record and confirmed the fact that he would be leaving with the prisoner, Daniel Ackermann, in tow on an eleven o'clock flight from Dublin flying to New York's JFK. For the remaining twenty-eight minutes, Tom Dawson did all the talking, answered the occasional question and presented the documents to the court.

"Short and sweet, just the way we like it," Dawson said as they stepped out into the main corridor and stood facing one another. Ann Dumphy remained a respectable four or five feet behind Dillon.

"You made it look so easy," Dillon said.

"I do a number of these in any given month. Believe me, this one was a breeze. They have a formality they have to go through, make sure all the 'i's are dotted and the 't's get crossed. A good deal depends on who is sitting on the bench on any given day. I've appeared in front of this guy before. He's good, gets to the point and moves things along. A couple of them, good Lord, you'd swear they've never done it before. By the way, compliments to whoever handled your paperwork. I had someone out of Kansas City a couple of months back, they ended up flying home empty-handed. As far as

I know, their guy is still cooling his heels back in Mountjoy. I'm afraid he'll be released if they don't get it corrected soon."

Dawson shot a quick glance over Dillon's shoulder at Ann Dumphy seeming to keep her distance. He looked a little disappointed, then said, "Hey, please don't take it personal, I'd love to stay and talk, but I've another appointment in about thirty minutes. You've got my number should you need anything. If I don't answer, contact the embassy's general number. They'll put you in touch with someone. Pleasure to meet you, Marshal. Ann, nice to see you, as always. We'll have to get together again sometime and maybe catch up. Give me a call. Thanks, gotta run," Dawson said and then hurried out the door.

"Busy guy," Dillon said as they watched Dawson hurry toward the door.

"Hmm-mmm, a call I don't intend to make," Ann said, but didn't comment any further. "Marshal, you've got the rest of the day for some relaxing and some sightseeing. I won't tell if you won't," she said and smiled. "Or I could drop you off at the Gresham if you like. "

"I don't want to put you out; you've been more than kind. I'm thinking of maybe doing a little looking around. You got any suggestions?"

"Depends on how crazy you want to be. I...."

"Nothing too crazy. I don't need to end up sharing a cell with this Ackermann clown."

She smiled at that, then said, "Tell you what. I'd have to change, but I could meet you at your hotel in a couple of hours, give you a little tour, maybe make some suggestions if you wanted to wander around tomorrow."

"Really? You'd do that?"

"I'd be more than happy to."

"God, I'd love it."

She glanced at her watch. "It's almost noon now. I could meet you in the lobby of the Gresham at two."

"That would be perfect. It'll give me an hour to close my eyes, and then I hopefully won't fall asleep before seven tonight."

"Fine." She smiled, then said, "'Casual' is the key word. Okay?"

"That's fine with me. I'll grab a taxi and plan on seeing you at the hotel at two. And thanks in advance. I'm looking forward to the afternoon."

"Okay, see you at two," she laughed. "In the hotel lobby." Then she headed off in the opposite direction. Dillon watched her strut away for a long moment before he flagged a taxi and headed back to his hotel.

Chapter Twelve

Dillon caught a quick nap and wandered down to the lobby about a quarter to two. Ann was already there, sipping a cup of tea. She looked beautiful wearing a pair of white shorts and a low-cut yellow top. As he approached he watched a couple of guys staring at her for a long moment as they strolled through the lobby and out the front door.

"Ann, you should have called my room instead of sitting down here alone. I was just up there twiddling my thumbs. Hey, by the way, you look absolutely fabulous."

She smiled, seemed to examine his attire from head to foot, then said, "Not bad yourself. Umm, what's with those jeans? You buy them like that or just lose a bet?"

He liked to think of his starched and pressed blue jeans as just one of the little imperfections that helped to make him perfect. "I send my jeans out to the dry cleaners. I like them starched and pressed. Holdover from some time I did in the army, I guess. Just trying to look my best for you."

"Mmm-mmm, that's definitely not on. I think I have a lot of work to do on you in the next twenty-four hours."

He let that last comment hang out there for a brief moment. "Oh, it'll take a lot longer than twenty-four hours to get me straightened out. I can be an awful lot of work."

She didn't so much as blink and said, "Then we best get started on the adventure. Come on, let's get you as big a taste of Dublin as we can cram into a short period of time."

It was a gorgeous afternoon and they walked about a half-block down O'Connell Street, then stopped at a small tourist office. Ann made arrangements for a bus tour while Dillon stopped and stared at the buildings around him. The street had basically been reduced to bombed-out rubble back in 1916, when the British shelled it during the Easter Rebellion. It had some great historical sites, although you'd never really know it and they were easy to walk past without ever having any idea. With the exception of the General Post Office across the street from where he stood, everything else was rather low-key. Or maybe everything was just over shadowed by the McDonald's, Burger King, Supermacs or Dr. Quirkey's Good Time Emporium.

"Tour's all set. Come on" Ann said, and Dillon dutifully followed her onto a red double-decker tour bus called 'Hop-On Hop-Off.' They climbed up to the second level and settled in the back behind a dozen Asian tourists who started taking photos with their cellphones before the bus had even begun to pull away from the curb.

"We can get off whenever you like," she said as the bus crossed the O'Connell Street bridge over the River Liffey. "But the entire route takes just a little over an hour, and we can ride the bus for free back to anything that looks interesting for the next twenty-four hours. So let's just sit back and enjoy ourselves and the rare sunshine."

"Sounds great," he said, and settled down to take in the sights and listen to the driver's narrative for the next hour. In between times they got to know a little bit more about one another.

It turned out she was the youngest of four girls, single, and originally from County Sligo out in the west of Ireland. She'd been in the Garda Síochána for seven years and lived on the north side of Dublin in an area called Drumcondra. "The north side of Dublin, it's where all the real Dubs live."

Reading between the lines, he guessed she was a bit of a workout freak, probably read the side panel on food containers to determine the fat and sugar content, and if you took her out to dinner she'd decline dessert, but then eat more than half of yours. She also seemed to possess a solid dose of common sense. Oh, and the white shorts were wonderfully tight. As she climbed the steps to the second level on the bus he was able to detect a very small thong.

They rode the bus for the entire route, then rode it back to the Guinness brewery. They took the tour and ended up drinking a pint of Guinness on the top floor of the brewery in the Gravity Bar, a fairly large circular bar with windows all the way around that let you see out as far as the Irish Sea and on this day was populated by a couple hundred tourists.

Fortunately, Ann knew the barman and they were able to grab two more pints, on the house. They hopped on the tour bus outside the brewery and rode it back to the city center.

The buildings started to look familiar and he could tell they were getting close to the hotel. He didn't really want the day to end so he said, "Hey, Ann, thanks for giving up the rest of your day to show me around Dublin. You've really got a beautiful city."

She smiled, then said, "it was so not a bother, actually my pleasure. It's been too long a while since I was at Guinness. They still pour some of the best pints in Dublin."

"Nice of the bartender to give us a couple of free ones. You said he's from your home town. Did you go to school with him or did you used to date him?" he asked, then immediately regretted the second question.

"Jimmy? Date him? Are you daft?" she laughed. "No, he dated one of my sisters though, at least for a time, before he moved here, to Dublin, like we all do when we turn seventeen."

"And your sister?"

She laughed again. "I think she took up with someone that same night, or maybe it was the next day. They're married now maybe nine or ten years with four boys and a large farm."

He thought back to his own youth, his parents' farm and the nonstop labor involved. "Sounds like a lot of work."

"The boys or the farm?"

"You kidding? Both. The farm work is twenty-four seven, and four boys, what one doesn't think of the others will."

"Mmm-mmm, you're telling me. They've one of the largest farms in the district."

"Oh?"

"Yeah, a full forty hectares."

"Hectares? What's forty hectares in acres?"

"I think nearly a hundred acres," she said, then looked at Dillon and apparently picked something up in his expression. "And you said you grew up on a farm? I suppose some ginormous American monstrosity twice the size of little old Ireland, and I bet you raised prize bulls and race horses."

"Not exactly. It's in the middle of the US, up against Canada, a place called Minnesota. We raised corn, soybeans, had a small dairy herd, some hogs, chickens for laying, nothing unusual for that part of the country."

"So how big is your parents' farm?"

"It's a thousand acres, so I guess it would be about, what? Four hundred hectares? Does that sound about right?"

She just shook her head and said, "Americans," in sort of a dismissive tone.

"My family homesteaded it back in the 1850s."

"Homesteaded?"

"In those days, before Minnesota became a state, if you lived on the land for five years, raised a crop and a family you could buy the land, a hundred and sixty acres, for cheap. The government wanted people on the land. So my grandparents, going back four greats, did just that. They were famine people from County Cork, left here in 1847, and ended up in Minnesota. They couldn't read or write. By the way, I'm sure Ireland was happy to see the back side of them, and with a hundred and sixty acres they ended up wealthier than they ever dreamed."

"The American dream," Ann said and smiled.

"Yeah, really. Although not without its difficulties. Winters, epidemics, wars, but they made it. Following generations purchased more land or acquired it through marriage. It was a great way to live and a great place to grow up, but in the end it wasn't for me. Still, I've a lot of fond memories."

She nodded, smiled, but didn't say anything. A few minutes later the bus pulled up to the curb and they climbed off. They sort of stood there on the sidewalk, like two rocks in the middle of a rushing stream, people hurrying past in either direction, the two of them seemingly at a loss for words.

"Well," Ann said, extending her hand, first to break the ice, and bring the awkward moment to a close. "I honestly enjoyed myself. Really I did."

"Hey, I don't mean to sound pushy, but do you have any dinner plans?" Dillon asked. He'd taken hold of her hand, and held on. "I mean, no problem if you do. I get it. But if you don't, I'd love to take you to dinner. It's the least I can do, you've really made this trip enjoyable. I think I've finally started to recover after my flight over and having to sit next to Mr. Nibbles."

"Oh, yeah, your girlfriend. The one in the pink moo-moo."

"Please, don't even mention her. I literally had nightmares about her and that little dog last night."

"You should find yourself a nice Irish girl," she said, then raised an eyebrow for just a brief moment, staring at Dillon for a second or two longer than might be normal.

"Well, do you know one who'd like to go somewhere for dinner?"

"I'd love to," she laughed.

"You pick the spot," he said, then realized he was still holding onto her hand.

Chapter Thirteen

Alexei Bazanov had received the phone call just a few minutes after two, not quite three hours after the perfunctory review of Dillon's paperwork and the signing of the release order authorizing Daniel Ackermann's flight back to the US with Marshal Dillon serving as escort.

He'd put off lunch in favor of this afternoon's entertainment, two sisters, Anka and Yana. At the moment he was in the process of pouring himself another chilled vodka while having difficulty remembering which sister was Anka and which one was Yana, not that he really cared or that it even mattered. He'd call them whatever he felt like.

The sisters had fled the Crimea eighteen months earlier. They'd traveled across the Ukraine, were smuggled into Poland and from there "worked" their way across the EU to Holland. They ended up working in Amsterdam, in the De Wallen, and quickly became local stars at one of Alexei's brothels. The sisters were popular, very popular as a matter of fact. At least up until the moment the Dutch authorities became suspicious about their passports and Alexei had to dispatch two of his staff for the better part of a week just to get the situation under control.

His team took the ferry from Dublin to the UK, drove down to Kent, then loaded their van on the Eurotunnel shuttle which brought them into France. From France they drove to Amsterdam and picked up the sisters once they'd finished with the evening's "appointments." By all reports they made their departure just twenty-four hours ahead of the Dutch police who, thankfully, returned too late to make an arrest.

Alexei tossed back another vodka while admiring the sisters who'd only just arrived this morning. He twirled his hand holding the empty glass to indicate the girls should display all sides of their attributes. He set his glass down on the marble-topped end table and proceeded to spoon a healthy portion of caviar onto a small piece of bread, which he promptly stuffed into his mouth, then clapped in appreciation of the performance. There would be money to be made here, lots of money.

The sisters were blonde, white blonde, with hair hanging down to the middle of their backs. Their icy blue eyes didn't so much invite as dare one to explore, and Alexei poured himself another chilled vodka, sipped and pondered the possibilities.

"Play with your sister, Anka. Excite her," he called out in Russian, then half-choked on his vodka when the smaller-breasted woman he thought was Anka struck a pose and her large-breasted sister, apparently the real Anka, began to fondle the smaller pair of breasts. Still, all in all, it was an excellent bit of entertainment and he downed his shot.

He poured himself another vodka, and made a mental note as to their names once again. He suddenly frowned when the door to the room opened. A barrel-chested man, built not unlike a large tree stump, in need of a shave, and a shower, headed across the room toward Alexei. He carried a silver tray, on which rested a cellphone. As Tree Stump approached he worked extremely hard not to leer at the two women, although he'd been watching through the crack between the double doors for the past half-hour.

"Your call has come through," he said in Russian, bending down ever so slightly and extending the silver tray with the phone toward Alexei. He positioned himself so that his back was to the women, although it was impossible not to hear their moans.

"Our contact?" Alexei asked, picking up the phone, and the man nodded. He pushed a button and in near perfect English asked, "You have information I requested?"

"I do. Same deal as before, twenty-five hundred quid, cash. That sound okay to you?"

"I really won't know until I hear what the information is you find so valuable, now will I?"

There was a long pause on the other end of the line. Yana, or was it Anka, had just grabbed her sister's breasts, the larger pair, and now they were both pulling, pinching and moaning, oblivious to Alexei talking on the phone. He set his glass of vodka down and rammed a finger into his ear. "What time?" he said, then shoved the finger just a little deeper as one of the women began to encourage her sister.

"Eleven o'clock. They're flying back to the States on Delta. Leaving from terminal two. This Sunday."

"Sunday?"

"Yeah. Delta, eleven o'clock. They'll be driving two vehicles and they may be armed."

"And under guard through the terminal?"

"Yes and no. They'll provide security but they don't enter the normal way. They'll actually drive around to the runway side of the concourse and enter through a special door. Two vehicles. They'll have someone blocking entry to the area for thirty minutes beforehand, and waving the two vehicles through. If you can get there before and be waiting for them that may be your best option."

"Good, very good, thank you," Alexei said, raising his voice slightly to talk over the moaning sisters. "Payment coming your way at the usual time and place," he said, then disconnected. *Be there waiting*, he thought. *No, that wasn't going to work.*

He placed the phone back on the silver tray, and to the tree stump, still with his back to the

84

sisters, said, "Get in touch with Borya Fedorov. I'll want to see him in two hours."

"As soon as you're finished here, very good."

Bazonav looked over at the sisters, the two of them clearly enjoying their frenzied activity, and he said, "No, wait, better make it three. Yes, tell him three hours, and then I'll want to see him."

The tree stump nodded and walked back toward the double doors. He opened the door then slowly pulled it closed, taking his time to watch the sisters who were now lying on the plush oriental rug enjoying one another's sexual proclivities, apparently focused solely on one another, and oblivious to Bazanov's enthusiastic clapping. Tree stump continued to stare through the crack between the doors.

Chapter Fourteen

Dillon was expecting meat and potatoes. Lots of potatoes. But the place Ann picked was a Thai restaurant called the Red Torch. They'd gotten off the tour bus on O'Connell Street, then walked across the Liffey, up past Trinity College and the Bank of Ireland on Dame Street. From there they entered into a maze of small, narrow, twisty, turning streets to a restaurant called the Red Torch.

It turned out to be the perfect choice. They leisurely devoured their meals along with a bottle of wine, talking back and forth and just, well, just learning about one another.

It was one of those pauses in conversation, not uncomfortable, just a pause after a wonderful meal. Dillon was swirling the last of his wine in his glass, wishing he wasn't flying out on Sunday and wishing there was at least one more glass of wine left in the bottle.

"Could you stand a bit of music?" she asked as the waiter appeared and began to clear their plates away.

"I'd love it. Did you want me to sing?"

"Actually, no. But we could head into Temple Bar, that's an area with lots of pubs, live music, some of it traditional. Or, if you're up for just a little longer walk, we could check out the Brazen Head. It's the oldest pub around and they've always got nice music there. Then, just after midnight, we could hop across the street to the Merchant; they've a fun band there tonight. I mean, that is if you're up for it. Whatever you feel like doing."

"I'd love to check out that Brazen Head place. But what do you say to maybe one more glass of wine here?"

"I could maybe be talked into just one more," she said and smiled.

"Two more glasses of wine for us, and then when you have a moment I'll grab the check, but no rush."

"Yes, sir," the waiter said and hurried off.

"Oh no, Jack, that's not right. Really, I can't let you pay for dinner. I'll get it, it's not a problem."

"Ann, I had the most wonderful day, and all because of you. Now, I'm the one who asked you to dinner, so I'm the one who's getting the check. You can sit there and just feel bad about the fact that I'm such a really, really nice guy, and maybe come up with a way to pay me back," he said and then let that last comment hang out there for a long moment.

She raised her eyebrows, smiled and said, "I'll have to think about that last line for a bit, but I'll be getting the pints at the Brazen Head. So do not even think about offering to pay. There, now we're settled, and not another word."

They finished their glasses of wine and were out the door twenty minutes later, walking down Dame Street past the Gaiety Theatre and Dublin Castle. They wove in and out of the sidewalk crowd and all sorts of people who were stopped and chatting. After a few minutes she linked her arm in Dillon's, gave it a tight squeeze and said, "We're really going to have to do something about those jeans you're wearing. They're so old fashioned, God, the look of you. I've never seen anything like it before."

"It's the way I am. I like my clothes to be squared away."

"Whatever," she said, looking at him and then sort of rolling her eyes. "Another one of those imperfections? I'm beginning to think there may be more than just a few."

They walked on for a few more blocks past Christ Church Cathedral, then down a hill. "That's it over there, across the street, the Brazen Head. It's billed as the oldest pub in all of Ireland. They've been pouring pints in there since 1198."

"Yeah, right."

"No, really, 1198."

"Get out of here. You mean to tell me that place has been a bar for more than three

88

hundred years before Columbus came to America? You gotta be kidding me."

"Wow. Just imagine, who would have ever thought there could be something like that in the world before America was discovered?" she laughed, and picked up her pace.

They entered a sort of courtyard with people drinking in an open air area off to the left and a couple of doors on the right-hand side. "Come on," she said, opening the second door and stepping in. "It's some of the best Guinness in town."

They stepped into a small room. The bar itself might have had room for four but certainly no more than six to sit comfortably. There were a handful of tables around the room with a small fireplace in the far corner. The ceiling looked to be about seven feet high and was completely covered with currency, as were all the walls. The currency was mostly dollar bills from what Dillon could tell, along with a few euros and yen, all emblazoned with signatures and dates written on them in black marker.

"Noel, a pint and a glass of Guinness," Ann said to the bartender.

Noel, the bartender, had a pair of glasses hanging round his neck and looked to be past retirement age. When he stepped out from behind the bar Dillon noticed he wore a gold chain around his wrist. He took Ann's hand in his, gracefully kissed it, then patted it as he spoke. "Nothing's too good for my favorite arresting officer," he said, and flashed a smile.

"Oh, Noel, you lovely man. You're too sweet. Now get me a Guinness, you knacker."

"At your service, madam."

"Noel," she said as he placed a glass beneath the tap and began to pour. "I'd like you to meet a friend of mine, Jack Dillon. Jack, this is my favorite barman, at least for the moment, Noel. Of course it all depends on how long I've to wait for my pint."

"Nice to meet you," Noel said. He then proceeded to fill their glasses a little more than two-thirds full. One of the glasses, presumably Ann's, was half the size of the other.

"Jack's a US Marshal," Ann said.

"Oh, so you've come all this way to arrest her. What's she done this time?"

"He can't tell you," Ann replied.

"So, do you ride a horse or what?" Noel asked. He didn't sound like he was trying to be funny.

"No, the Marshals Service is just another branch of law enforcement in the States. We're a little more national in our scope."

"You carrying a gun?"

"It's against the law here," Dillon said and smiled. At that point Noel took three steps to the far end of the bar and took another order, leaving their Guinness glasses about two-thirds full. "What about our drinks?" Dillon asked Ann.

"Perfection can't be rushed. You pour Guinness at a forty-five-degree angle until you're halfway up the gold harp on the side of the Guinness glass, then you set the glass

90

down and let it settle. Once it's settled, you top it off, keeping the glass level. You always want the foam to rise up just above the rim of the glass. That makes the perfect Guinness pour."

"What if your glass doesn't have that harp on it?"

She gave Dillon a strange look. Clearly his question hadn't registered. "That's a Guinness glass. They all have harps. It's the only glass you'd use to pour a pint of Guinness."

"Yeah, but what if you have a different glass, like a Budweiser glass or a beer mug or something? What if the bar is really busy and the barman just reaches for the closest glass?"

"That sort of thing wouldn't happen here," she said, shaking her head. "Pour a Guinness into the wrong glass? You'd be crazy. And if it did happen, I'd leave the bar, never go back, and I'd be duty bound to tell everyone I knew that the place was run by a madman."

Noel set their glasses on the bar, then pushed the full pint toward Ann.

"I'm just having the glass," she said, and reached for the half-pint.

"Oh, are we pretending to act the lady tonight, or still in recovery from an earlier soiree?" he said.

"Funny, not." She laughed, then turned toward Dillon. "Let's check out the music scene. Thanks, Noel. Great to see you again."

"Nice to meet you," Dillon said.

Noel smiled, raised an eyebrow and nodded at Ann. "She's a special one. Take care of her."

Dillon nodded back, then followed Ann out of the room and into another one that was only slightly larger and crammed with about ten times the people. Standing room only. The band was in the middle of playing "*Rock Me, Mama, Like a Wagon Wheel'*"- not exactly what Dillon thought of as traditional Irish music, but just as fun. He gave a loud whistle at the end of the song.

Ann leaned into his ear and said, "This band is called the Brazen Hussies. They play down here every weekend and then the occasional off night."

They stayed at the Brazen Head, enjoying the music, the Guinness and the crowd until a little after midnight. Once the band finished their final number the crowd cheered and clapped. Ann had to draw close to Dillon's ear so he could hear her. "Let's go across the street to the Merchant. It's always gas," she said. They finished their Guinness. Left via the room Noel was working in to say their good-byes then hurried out the door and across the street to O'Shea's Merchant. A rank of a half-dozen taxis waited outside the Brazen Head for fares.

Chapter Fifteen

Borya Fedorov arrived at Alexei's mansion as directed, exactly three hours after he had received the call. Then he waited almost another hour in the hallway outside Alexei's office. He was seated on an uncomfortable antique couch just opposite the grand staircase listening to a grandfather clock tick and then grind and chime every fifteen minutes. While he waited he studied the gold-framed paintings on the wall, not the technique or the colors but the scenes. Russian scenes, trees without leaves, windswept fields and snow. Not that he cared about art. No, Borya wondered where he could get one, a painting. Could he steal them from some rich bastard's home? Maybe, while he was at it, grab some silver from a cabinet or jewels from a bedroom.

He was young, his twenty-third birthday still a good month away. At a muscular five-feet-ten he was eager to please, and he viewed this summons as his first chance, quite possibly his only chance, to gain favor and attention. If he was honest with himself he was prepared to do whatever it would take, he would do absolutely anything, to gain the favor, and the respect of his boss, Alexi Bazanov.

Thus far he'd been assigned the tasks of an errand boy; pick up a case of vodka, collect a payment, deliver a woman to a customer, pick up a woman from a customer. He'd washed cars, picked up food, stood guard, opened doors, and been bored and frustrated out of his mind. But he'd never given up.

Whatever this particular summons was about, Borya had the feeling it was a major chance to prove his value. This had to be a shortcut, a way to gain a major step up the ladder. He was eager to please, and not about to miss the opportunity.

He replayed the phone call over and over again in his mind, hearing deep voice on the other end of the line. He wasn't even sure who it was that actually made the call, although he had his suspicions. "Mr. Bazanov would like to see you in three hours," the voice had said, just as simple as that, and then hung up. Borya had immediately rolled out of bed, quickly dressed and hurried home, leaving his partner at the time with a most unsatisfied look on her face and shouting he would not be welcome for a return visit.

Who cares? he thought. Going the places he was suddenly destined for, he could get two women, better-looking, and they'd be more than happy to pay him just for the privilege.

Yeah, with just the snap of his fingers he'd pick two from the long line of hopefuls.

So, when he heard activity in the upstairs hallway and then a voice, Borya jumped to his feet. Alexei eventually appeared and strolled down the stairs clad in an ankle-length navy-blue velvet robe with white silk lapels. He was filing his fingernails and appeared to be unaware of Borya standing at the bottom of the staircase looking hopeful.

The robe was loosely cinched around Alexei's waist with a matching navy-blue velvet belt. There was an embroidered gold crest over the right breast of the robe. As Alexi drew closer Borya noticed that the crest appeared to be an exact match to the crests embroidered on the navy-blue velvet slippers Alexei wore. Borya, having never heard of the designer Emilio Pucci let alone his crest, simply assumed the crest had something to do with Alexei's exalted station in life, the royalty he must have descended from, and it all seemed to make perfect sense. The man was literally a king, and now he wanted to meet with Borya.

Alexei slowly descended the stairs continuing to file his nails. He stopped on the bottom step, looked up at Borya as if taking notice for the very first time, then flashed a post-coital smile in his direction.

His hair, shaved on the sides and long on top, was still wet after just stepping out of the shower with the two sisters. The girls had run their hands through it in an effort to convince him to stay and it now appeared unkempt. He stood on the bottom step of the staircase, and gave a long sigh, waiting as Borya cautiously approached. Alexi held his hand out in a limp-wristed manner and Borya gently took hold with a shaking hand and focused on the heavy gold ring.

Addressing him in Russian, the young man said, "Thank you for calling me. I'm at your service and ready to accomplish whatever task you wish. I'll do whatever it takes." Then he lifted the hand to his lips, kissed the gold ring and looked up into Alexi's face.

Alexei looked him in the eye, gave a slight smile, closed his eyes and simply nodded.

Borya noticed what looked like a series of fresh scratches running across Alexei's chest before disappearing beneath his robe. There were four scratches, actually, quite possibly from finger nails. The skin appeared red and slightly raised. He was a about to say something, then thought it best not to make a comment.

"I hope I haven't kept you waiting too long. I was, ummm, detained, unfortunately…on a phone call. Yes, a very important phone call. Business, I'm afraid. I do appreciate your patience. You are Boris?" Alexei asked, and Borya felt himself begin to deflate.

"Actually, it's Borya. Borya Fedorov, sir. And I'm more than able to wait the few minutes, sir. I'm honored that you sent for me. I stand ready to serve you in whatever way you require and I can assure you I will never mention the slightest word."

Alexei smiled. The eagerness was exactly what he'd been looking for. "Come, please join me in my office," he said, and stepped off the staircase. He was suddenly barely shoulder height to young Borya, who followed him into the office like an anxious puppy, almost nipping at his heels, and ignoring the faint scent of perfume wafting from Alexei Bazanov's velvet robe.

Alexei walked around to the far side of the massive wooden desk and pulled his black leather chair back. Then, remembering the paddling he'd recently received from sisters Anka and Yana, he decided it might make a better impression if he simply remained standing.

"You've impressed me, Borya, as someone who would work hard to get ahead in our organization. I believe you may be someone who's not content with simply running errands any longer and you may be ready for a greater…shall we say, 'responsibility.'"

"I'll do whatever you wish, and I'll do it better than anyone else," Borya said. "If you'll just give me the chance, I'll show you what I'm capable of doing. I know you won't be disappointed."

Alexei smiled, nodded, then said, "You're about to get your chance."

Chapter Sixteen

"That's traditional music in that door," Ann said as Dillon was about to enter the Merchant bar. They'd just walked all of about fifty feet across the street from the Brazen Head. Dillon could hear the sound of a fiddle and an accordion playing inside.

She walked past the door and headed toward the corner of the building. "Come on, Jack. We'll go in down here, it's a little more crazy. Bit of a knocking shop, I guess you could say."

"A knocking shop? You mean like there's fights and shit?"

She gave him a quick look, then realized it wasn't translating. "No, not fights, a pick-up place, or a meat market I think you'd say in the States."

"A pick-up place? Are you looking for anyone in particular or just checking out your options?"

"I suppose you might say I'm just doing some comparison shopping, Mr. Smarty-

Pants," she said then pulled the door open. "Hi, Paul," she called as she stepped in and nodded at the burly bouncer with a shaved head.

"Annie," he said, then gave Dillon a close look from head to toe and back up again. He was a guy of average height, broad-shouldered and barrel-chested. He had bulging biceps, massive forearms and looked like he pumped iron for more than a few hours every day. A large, blue tattoo of some sort of Celtic-style design covered the better part of both forearms. "Intimidating" was one word that sprang immediately to mind. Dillon figured it was probably a pretty safe bet there wouldn't be a lot of trouble on his watch, and he held out his hand to shake. Paul took it and gave a gentle shake in return. For his part, Dillon felt like he was squeezing a brick.

More Guinness. By this time in the evening Dillon was in the process of using the local lingo. "A pint and a glass," he said, ordering their next round of Guinness. He didn't even have to say "Guinness," the barman just seemed to automatically know what he was talking about. He poured the drinks, a good three-minute process filling the glasses to a certain level then letting the contents settle for a couple of minutes before topping them up and sliding them across the bar to Dillon.

The room was wall-to-wall people, quite a few of them crowding the dance floor and no one apparently feeling any pain. The band was assembled on a small raised platform, maybe a foot high and positioned just next to the door. Dillon and Ann danced to a couple of songs, and Dillon noticed Ann was turning more than a few heads as she swayed and moved in time to the music.

The white shorts, the yellow top exposing a healthy cleavage, and the way she moved didn't leave a whole lot to the imagination. On the other side of the coin, if anyone looked at Dillon dancing it would have been more with pity or disgust than anything else. Dancing not on the top of the list of things he enjoyed doing.

They'd been in the place for a good hour, and if memory served they were on their third round of Guinness, make that the third round at the Merchant.

They were standing at the edge of the dance floor, watching the crowd dance. Some guy suddenly staggered over and asked Ann to dance, which struck Dillon as a bit strange. The guy was glassy-eyed, wove back and forth and replanted his feet a couple of times in a failed effort to maintain his balance.

At the time Dillon was standing with his arm around her shoulder. Ann had her arm around his waist. The question had interrupted their kiss, and by the way, not the first kiss of the late evening. She shook her head no, and the look on her face suggested a number of other comments.

The following series of events seemed to happen in just a matter of seconds.

The drunk called her a bitch. Dillon politely suggested he leave, followed up by the suggestion he, "Get the fuck out of here."

The drunk pushed Dillon, hard. Dillon calmly handed his pint of Guinness to Ann, then spun round and decked the bastard. His two friends jumped in. One of them punched Dillon with a right cross. Ann dropped the other one to the floor with a well-placed solid kick between the legs, all the while not spilling so much as a drop from either of their Guinness glasses.

Dillon grabbed the guy who punched him and the next thing he knew, Paul, the burly bouncer, had to pull him off. The guy was looking pretty bloody on the floor and Dillon's right hand was awfully sore. Oh yeah, and all three of them happened to be Americans. Naturally.

"You're liable to have a black eye before morning," Ann said not for the first time and laughed. They were seated on a pair of stools at a small back bar. She took a sip of her Guinness, then sort of tied a bar towel around a fresh bunch of ice cubes the bartender had just given her and handed it back to Dillon.

"Bunch of idiots," he said, took a long sip of Guinness and pressed the fresh ice pack up against the side of his face. "Nice kick you gave that bastard. It hurt just watching."

"Comes with the job. Besides, I liked it. How come you didn't want to press any charges? We could have made life miserable for the three of them for the next few days. Assaulting an Officer of the Law, they could have been locked up for a month, banned from ever returning here."

"I don't know if that would work, me being in American law enforcement. I think…."

"I was talking about me."

"Oh, yeah, of course. Still, all in all it would probably be best if my name wasn't associated with a barroom brawl. I've got a pain-in-the-ass boss who would like nothing better than to hang me with some sort of trumped-up international incident that reflects poorly on the service."

"Well, I think we better finish our Guinness, then get you home and get that swelling taken care of," she said, at which point burly bouncer Paul suddenly arrived with two more glasses of Guinness.

"On the house, for the two of yous. Thanks for the entertainment."

"Yeah, I noticed the band didn't even stop playing," Dillon said.

"That's 'cause you were sort of punching in time to the music. Great bit of a kick there, Annie. Would have been a goal for sure if you'd been out on the pitch."

"Thanks, Paul. It was my pleasure."

"Remind me to be careful around the likes of you from now on," he said, then wandered back to his post near the front door.

They finished their pints, had one more, or was it two? Then headed out the door and flagged a taxi.

Chapter Seventeen

They rode in the back of the taxi, sitting close to one another in the rear seat, very close. Dillon sat there with the bar towel and a fresh set of ice cubes pressed against his left eye, while Ann acted the part of the nurse. Although she seemed to be paying more attention to his thigh rather than his eye, running her hand slowly back and forth along his starched jeans. He wasn't about to ask her to stop.

"Bit of excitement, was it?" the taxi man asked as he studied Ann in the rearview mirror.

"A couple, three knackers," Ann said, then leaned over and kissed Dillon's hand holding the ice pack.

"Of course they happened to be Americans," Dillon added.

"Heard a couple of auld wans chatting about it on the way out. Sounds like you gave em what for."

"I could have done without the excitement," Dillon said.

The driver nodded, studied Ann for another moment then directed his attention back to the road.

"Just up there on the right, past that parked car," she said ten minutes later as the taxi wound its way down the darkened lane. The lane was narrow, tree-lined, and sort of wove through a neighborhood of identical, two-story attached homes, four or five to a group. The structures were stucco, with tiled roofs and a small wall no more than three feet high running next to the front sidewalk. A number of cars were parked along the lane, pulled halfway up over the curb and onto the sidewalk.

They were both out of the taxi and watching it pull away before it dawned on Dillon that they weren't at the Gresham Hotel.

"Come on, let's get that looked at," Ann said, then opened the front gate and pulled a set of keys from her purse. She seemed to fumble with the keys for a moment before she unlocked the door. She gave a quick smile in Dillon's direction, then stepped inside and quickly entered a code into the alarm system keypad mounted on the wall. Once the alarm stopped beeping she closed the door behind them and said, "There, now that's settled."

The front hallway was small by American standards, but neat, with a door on either end and a staircase running up to the second floor along the outside wall. He followed her maybe ten feet to the far end of the hall and through an open door. She clicked on lights, illuminating an extremely neat kitchen and dining area.

The kitchen cabinets were lightly stained oak with brass handles. Shiny, black granite countertops ran against a far wall and over an island that essentially separated the cooking area from the dining area. The dining table was oak, thick oak, with six matching chairs placed around it and a matching sideboard resting against the far wall. The four-burner range was inset in what looked like a former fireplace and lined with more black granite. Two ovens with windows in the doors rested below the range.

Ann threw her house keys on the granite countertop, dropped her purse on a stool at the end of the kitchen counter, and said, "Here, give me that towel, Gimpy, and I'll get you some fresh ice for that eye, see if we can't keep the swelling down."

"It's okay, you don't have to...."

"Listen, Mister, you're not the one who has to look at you. Now give," she said, then flashed a sexy smile, raised an eyebrow, and Dillon immediately surrendered the soggy bar towel to her, now fairly well-soaked with just the slightest hint of ice left in it.

She set the towel in the kitchen sink, then pulled a fresh one out of the drawer, pulled an ice tray out of the freezer and set four ice cubes on the towel. "Here, wrap this up and get it on that bruise. God, the knackers, the three of them. For feck's sake."

Dillon folded the edges of the towel over, then placed it against his cheek.

"That's much better. God, I don't know about you, but I'm famished. Fancy something to eat? Maybe eggs and some toast? A little glass of vino, oh, and I've got a craving for some rashers. Sound like a plan?"

"Sounds perfect. What can I do to help?"

"You can set the table when I pass you the silverware, otherwise stay out of my way," she said and smiled.

He sat at the kitchen counter while she bustled around cooking the eggs and rashers. She'd taken what appeared to be a loaf of homemade bread out of the refrigerator, cut four slices and placed them in the toaster. She placed a bottle of white wine on the kitchen counter and trusted Dillon enough to pour two glasses for them.

Breakfast was ready in less than ten minutes. They ate, chatted, sipped wine, and enjoyed each other's company. She topped up her glass of wine while Dillon washed the dishes and the pan. She lingered around the last swallow of wine for a good ten minutes and suddenly seemed sort of removed, like she had something else on her mind. Dillon was just about to ask her to call a cab when she finished the glass in one large swallow, then took him by the hand and said, "Come on."

She turned the lights off in the kitchen and he followed her up the stairs.

"Bathroom's here, at the end of the hall. I'll leave the light on in case you're up in the middle of the night," she said, turning on the bathroom light and only partially closing the door.

"Here's the master bedroom," she said, walking past him, grabbing his hand as she did so. As they stepped into the bedroom she suddenly turned and faced him. "Do you think I'm too forward?"

"No, not at all," he said, thinking, *This is working out just fine.*

She smiled at that, turned on a small lamp that sat on a bedside table, then turned off the overhead light in the room and closed the door. The room was suddenly dim and she looked up into his eyes, moved closer, smiled and said, "God, but you're an absolute mess."

"Gee, thanks for that."

"I just meant that eye. I'm thinking it might just need some *very special* attention. And, well, then there's those jeans of yours. My God, starched. What the hell were you even thinking?" she said, then reached down and undid his belt….

Chapter Eighteen

She was seated at her dining room table, going through Twitter feeds on her cellphone. It was a physical exercise, moving her finger, giving her some mode of activity while she pondered exactly what she was going to say when he eventually entered the kitchen. She could hear him moving around up in the bedroom, so it was only a matter of time.

She wore her silk robe. It was short, barely down to her thighs, and rose-colored. She'd nothing on underneath, and as she heard him coming down the stairs she pulled it open ever so slightly, exposing just a little more cleavage. She pretended it was just an everyday occasion, lounging around half-naked. She took a deep breath, focused on her phone and hoped he wouldn't hear her heart pounding madly.

Dillon entered the kitchen dressed in the wrinkled shirt he'd worn the night before and the starched jeans. As he entered the room he immediately smelled coffee, and his stomach gave a long, loud growl in response.

"Mmm-mmm, hungry, are we? Help yourself to some coffee. I hope it's not too strong, I rarely make it. How did you sleep?" she asked without bothering to look up from her cellphone.

"Just like a baby, I woke up and cried every twenty minutes."

She quickly turned toward him, stared for a long moment before it dawned on her that he was joking, and the stress immediately left her. "Oh God, you are such an idiot. Go on, help yourself to some coffee. I put a mug out for you over on the counter. How's that eye feeling this morning? Fancy some ice for another cold pack?"

"It's fine."

"It doesn't look all that fine. Come here and let me see," she said, and set her cellphone on the table.

He bent down, and she studied the eye for a long moment, looking at it closely, turning his head from side to side. There was no hiding it. It was swollen, black and blue, and the white of his eyeball appeared bloodshot. "He got you a good one," she said, then kissed him. "But not so bad. I guess it could be worse. Better grab some coffee."

"I, umm, wanted to thank you for last night. It was really wonderful," he said, heading toward the coffee.

"Yeah, the Brazen Hussies and that band playing at the Merchant were both pretty good.

I have to say, it's been a while since I was in the Merchant. I like the place, in small doses."

"I wasn't talking about the bands, Ann. I meant, you know, when we got here, and upstairs."

She seemed to take a deep breath and smiled. "Yeah, about last night, just so you know. I've never, ever done anything like that before."

"What? Kicked a guy between the legs?"

She closed her eyes for a moment, shook her head, gave an exasperated sigh, and said, "Jesus, just get your coffee before *you* get the kick between the legs."

They had a leisurely breakfast of eggs and rashers, a repeat of the feast when they'd arrived six hours earlier. After breakfast she showered, dressed, and they walked the half-block to the bus stop at the top of the lane. They took the bus back into the city center and got off just across O'Connell Street from the GPO, maybe a half-block from Dillon's room at the Gresham Hotel.

"I'm going to pick up a couple of things. You can go back to your hotel room and get sorted. How about I meet you in front of the GPO in about an hour and a half, and we can sightsee or do whatever you'd like this afternoon. Sound like a plan?"

"Sounds great. I'll see you in front of the GPO in an hour and a half," Dillon said, repeating her instructions. "No rush. Do what you want to do and don't worry if you're running late. I'm enjoying just watching the people walking past and looking around."

"I'm always on time. See that you are," she said with a smile, then leaned against him, kissed him and hurried down the street.

He watched her as she waited at the curb for the traffic to pass. When it was all clear she hurried across the street toward the spire, a large stainless steel, needle-like monument where Nelson's Pillar had once stood. She turned once, saw him still watching and gave a quick wave, then blended into the crowd crossing the street and disappeared.

Dillon turned and headed up O'Connell Street toward the Gresham Hotel, thinking, *An afternoon with her in bed at the Gresham is all the sightseeing I'm interested in.*

Thirty minutes later he was shaved, showered and had a different shirt on with an hour to spare, and so he headed back out of the hotel. He ended up in Easons bookstore, just a block down from the GPO, wandering around aimlessly paging through books for the better part of an hour before he hurried out and up the street toward the GPO. He saw Ann coming around the corner with an armful of shopping bags just as he reached the GPO. He watched her for a moment, thinking about how beautiful she looked before she noticed him, waved, then sort of frowned.

"I don't believe it. You're still wearing those dreadful starched jeans with the crease?"

"I guess I could have put my suit back on, but I thought that might be a little too much. No doubt you've purchased nothing but necessary items," he said, looking at the bags. One of them was bright pink with the name *Ann Summers* printed across it in bold white letters.

She flashed a quick smile, then said, "I just wanted to see if you'll be able to live up to your nickname."

"My nickname?"

"We'll get into that later. Not to worry, I don't think you'll be complaining. Come on, I want to show you something," she said, then linked her arm in Dillon's, and they headed back the way she'd come down Henry Street.

Some years back Henry Street had been converted to a broad pedestrian walkway, with shops on either side. They'd only traveled a short distance when Dillon spotted the F. X. Buckley butcher shop just off on Moore Street and he hurried over to look in the window.

Trays of different meats were arranged in the window. Some of the meats were substantially different from what he was used to back in the States. There were three or four skinned rabbits, an entire hog's head, a beef tongue, and a half-dozen quail, all staring back at him. Inside the shop, four geese hung from the ceiling. The floor was coated with a layer of sawdust, and the customers were two-deep at the counter. The half-dozen butchers wore white hats, with blue and white pinstriped aprons over their white butcher's coats. All the butchers wore a white shirt and tie. Dillon stood there and stared for a couple of long minutes enjoying the view.

Finally Ann said, "It's a butcher shop. What's the big deal?"

"It's just different than what I'm used to, nice to see. It's like something from a hundred years ago."

"Well, speaking of nice to see, come on. Right now we need to take care of something before I lose my mind."

"Take care of something?"

"Just come on," she said, then linked her arm in Dillon's again and steered him out of the butcher shop. They walked down Henry Street arm in arm and into a large department store where she directed him up an escalator and into the men's department. "You're not leaving here until you get a new pair of jeans. Proper jeans, thank you. And then you're not allowed to leave here unless you're wearing them."

"But these are fine. They…."

"Just one quick question before you continue with your nonsense. Did you enjoy yourself before you fell asleep last night and snored my ear off until I got out of bed?"

"Well, umm, yeah, I told you it was really nice."

"Would you be interested in a repeat performance? Think you might be able to handle that sort of activity two days in a row, or would you prefer to walk the streets of Dublin on your own?"

"You bet I can handle it. Of course, ummm, great idea. In fact, I was thinking maybe we should...."

"Don't think, just pick out a proper pair of jeans and take those manky things you're wearing back to the States and burn them. I'm buying by the way, so you've absolutely no excuse."

"You don't have to do...."

"Oh please, I insist. Believe me, it's so not a problem. I've a reputation to protect, and if we're going to be seen together we need to do something about...." She glanced down, then raised her eyebrows and stared at his jeans for a moment and shook her head. "Go ahead, you can pick out any pair you want. I have right of first refusal. Now get to it," she said, then crossed her arms and smiled.

Arguing did not seem to be the wiser choice at the moment, so he started sorting through stacks of jeans. To say he was out of the demographic would be an understatement. He might purchase a pair of jeans once every other year, and then at a large building supply store where he only had to pay about fifteen bucks for a pair.

Sorting through the stacks, one pair seemed worse than the next. Relaxed fit, normal fit, tight fit, flared, straight, he shook his head in disgust. Most of of the jeans looked like someone had nailed them to a bench and then taken a belt sander to the things. They were torn across the knees, or had little designs embroidered on the back pockets.

"Why would anyone pay money for new jeans that look so worn you'd throw them out?"

"Have you found a pair yet?"

"No, they all…."

"Then keep looking, Mister."

"Look at this, sequins? On guys' jeans? I wouldn't stand a chance wearing these back in the States."

"Mmm-mmm, yeah, probably best to skip those. They won't do. Like I said, keep looking."

"But I…."

"Remember, there's a reward."

"This pair will be great. Let's get them," he said, and pulled a pair in his size off the next closest stack.

She held them out in front of her for a moment, examining, turning them round, checking the rear, then back to reexamine the front. "Okay, now let's have you try them on."

He shook his head. There were limits to what he was going to do. "Ann, I'm a guy. We don't try this stuff on, we just know the size is going to fit and it almost always does. And if it doesn't, who cares? It'll just be off by a little."

"Remember the reward," she said, then smiled and shook her head back and forth.

What the hell, it would only take a minute to try them on. He hurried over into one of the dressing rooms and closed the door. A full-length mirror hung on the back of the door. He quickly hung his starched jeans up on a hook, then stepped into the new pair. They felt well-worn as he pulled them on, too worn. He stared in the dressing room mirror and thought they looked like something even he would have tossed out. Some poor guy in China was probably paid to wear them twenty-four hours a day, every day, for three months. Both legs had slits across the thigh. And people pay money for this? He buttoned the waist, zipped the fly and walked back out to Ann standing next to a large mirror. He figured he'd let her get a taste of just how stupid they looked.

"Oh, wow, I like that. Don't they feel a lot better than those stiff-as-a-board things you had on you?"

"No, not really. Please tell me you're kidding, Ann. You can't actually like these. The things look like someone already threw them away. I mean, look, they've got slits in the legs here and they're supposed to be new. Not to mention they have you paying extra for...."

"You serious?" She looked around for anyone nearby, then half-whispered, "Come on, let's get them and go back to your hotel room. I want to just eat you alive."

"Maybe we should get two pairs?"

"One will be enough to start."

"Okay, let me go get changed and I'll be right back."

"Keep them on and leave that pair you wore in here hanging in the dressing room."

He gave her a smile and walked back to the dressing room, thought about his reward, and left the jeans with the slits on. As she paid for his new pair of jeans, he asked the clerk for a

116

bag to put the old pair in. Ann just rolled her eyes and shook her head.

"Oh my," the clerk said, stuffing the jeans into the bag, noticing for the first time the sharp crease and feeling the starch. "Whatever happened here?" she said and gave a puzzled look.

"Americans," Ann said by way of explanation and just left it at that.

The clerk nodded in a way that suggested, "Say no more."

Back in his hotel room, she set her bags on the desk, then set the pink bag with the white letters that spelled out *Ann Summers* on its side and pulled out a battery-operated device. "They do call you 'Dildo,' don't they?" she laughed.

Once he'd lived up to his nickname and collected his reward they both fell asleep.

"How long have we been asleep?" she asked sometime later, then yawned and snuggled next to him. She was still wearing a small gold crucifix along with a very satisfied smile.

"A good hour-plus, it's close to five."

"What, we slept away the afternoon?"

"Not entirely. Besides, you earned a rest."

"So maybe you're beginning to realize *Ann Summers* isn't all that bad?"

"I didn't know it was a toy store for ladies. How'd I do?"

"Hmm-mmm, very good. I'm a very happy lady. And you?"

"I'm very well taken care of, thank you."

"What do you feel like doing now?"

"Oh, I don't know, maybe another round with Ann…."

"I think it might be nice if I was able to get some feeling back in my legs first. Fancy doing anything tonight?" she said,

"I would like to take you out to dinner, somewhere unique. I have to be on that flight tomorrow morning with that jerk banker, Ackermann. What do you say to making tonight special, something for us to remember? A nice restaurant, have a fun meal, no craziness, just the two of us."

She seemed to think about that for a long moment while twirling a finger on his chest, then she sort of half-rose on her elbow and said, "You know, I'm, I'm not a slapper."

"What?"

"I said, I'm not a slapper. I guess it means a slut in American. After last night and now this afternoon you probably think I am, but I've never done anything like this before. I…."

"I believe you," he said, and pushed a finger to her lips to stop her from saying anything more. She kissed his finger and snuggled up against his chest. He held her tightly and they remained in that position for a long while, wondering if they'd ever see one another after tomorrow.

After a long while Ann quietly climbed out of the bed and headed for the bathroom. She remained in there for quite a while. He was debating about knocking on the door to see if she was okay when he heard it open. She

118

stepped into the room, still naked, and said, "How does Chapter One sound?"

Chapter Nineteen

They headed out for a late dinner at place called Chapter One. The restaurant was two blocks up from the Gresham Hotel, just past Parnell Square. The evening had begun to cool off and there was a slight breeze. They'd walked up to the restaurant holding hands, weaving through all the foot traffic like a pair of fish swimming upstream. They crossed the street at a stoplight and headed toward the building labeled "Writers Museum." Out front at the Hugh Lane Gallery was a light display of a figure walking with a cane, and Dillon at first thought that was a rather strange sign for a restaurant.

"That's the restaurant?"

"No, that's an art gallery. The restaurant is right here."

"Where?"

It turned out they were standing directly in front of the place. Ann was looking at the stairs that led down to the lower level entry. "You sure you don't mind?" Ann asked after a long moment. "I mean, it's a five-star restaurant, it's pretty pricey, and we may not even get in without a reservation. It's a really popular place and it's Saturday night. I don't know, maybe. ..."

"Maybe let's think positive. I'm hungry. You're really worth it, and we're here, so let's give it a try," he said and headed down the steps. They walked into a small, very quiet bar, with just three couples. Two couples were seated at different tables and another sat at the bar.

"Folks?" the barman asked.

"Hoping we can get a table," Dillon said, then added, "We don't have a reservation."

"Not a problem, we'll get you taken care of."

"Hello," a young woman said from behind him just a moment later.

Dillon turned and said, "Table for two?"

"Sure thing, this way," she said and led them into a back dining room. "I like those jeans," she said looking at Dillon as she pulled out a chair for Ann, then set two menus for them on the table.

Ann just smiled and said, "See."

They were seated at a small table in the far corner of the dining room. The room was dimly lit, with tables not too close together, intimate in a nicely casual way. Since it was on the lower level the exterior walls consisted of large blocks of stone. Dillon guessed the structure had to be at least a hundred and fifty years old.

Dark, heavy timbers ran across the ceiling and were embedded in the stone walls.

They looked at the menus, ordered and then chatted about everything and nothing until their first course arrived maybe fifteen minutes later. They ate a leisurely four-course meal with wine, but not too much wine. As it turned out, that was probably a very good thing based on the direction the dinner conversation began to head.

Dillon hadn't eaten since breakfast and he'd wolfed down his first course the moment it arrived, a small tomato salad. All the salad seemed to do was stimulate his appetite, and he was in the process of thinking about licking the plate clean when things began to take a turn. Ann had a second spoonful of her onion broth and then set her spoon down on the table.

"You don't like it? You want something else?"

"No. It's fine, very good as a matter of fact. I just want to say something to you."

"Okay," he said, setting his fork down and folding his hands in front of him. His defenses immediately started to go up as he felt the atmosphere at their table begin to cool down.

"First of all…."

He wasn't sure where this was going, other than not his way. Anytime a woman began a conversation with the words "first of all," experience had taught him he really didn't have a snowball's chance in hell. Over the years he'd had dozens of conversations that

122

started like this and he couldn't recall even one that had gone in his favor, ever.

"...I'd just like to say I've had a really wonderful time. I've enjoyed your company and being with you and even the *incident* at the Merchant, I loved it all. To be honest, I wasn't all that thrilled with being handed the assignment of keeping you...."

"I was an assignment?" he said, not meaning to sound quite so incredulous, hoping the expression on his face didn't match the tone of his voice. Great, he was an assignment, like who was going to be stuck working the weekend and shuttling the stupid American around.

"Would you please just let me finish?" she said and looked at him for a very long moment before she continued. "Now, as I was saying, I wasn't thrilled with the assignment of having to watch over you to make sure you didn't embarrass the United States of America too much and that you didn't do substantial damage to little old Ireland along the way. We never quite know what to expect when we have one of you to deal with."

"To deal with?"

"If I could be allowed to finish, please."

"You seem to have kept me out of trouble, mostly," he said. He paused without going into any further detail, and sort of ran a finger over his black and swollen eye.

"As I was saying, I've really enjoyed our time together. Despite you picking fights at the

Merchant with other Americans, it's been a really wonderful weekend."

"Hey, I'm not sure where you're going with this. Let me just say I've enjoyed it at least as much as you, and probably more. And as for that situation at the Merchant, it really was your fault. If you hadn't been so drop dead gorgeous those fools wouldn't have looked twice. Who can blame them for acting stupid? Nice kick by the way. Oh, and without trying to embarrass you," he said, then leaned forward and lowered his voice to almost a whisper, "The sex was absolutely wonderful, and I not only don't think you're a slapper, I happen to think you are really a very, very wonderful woman. I have to leave tomorrow, but I'd like to come back sometime and see you. Sometime soon."

She seemed to sort of sigh, then said, "Yes, I'd like to see you again *sometime*, too." Then she looked away, picked up her spoon and had another bit of onion broth. She continued to look around the room, looking at anything as long as it wasn't Dillon.

"Did I say something wrong? Look, Ann, I'm a guy, I have one switch, it just says 'on' and 'off.'"

"No, no, you didn't say anything wrong, Jack. Apparently I just can't quite compartmentalize the way you can. I'm simply not able for it. Not to worry. I don't mean that as a criticism, unfortunately, it's just a fact. It would seem to appear I just think about things more than you."

"And the duck breast," the server said, suddenly appearing and placing a plate down next to Ann. "The wood pigeon terrine, sir," he said, laying a plate down in front of Dillon. "Pepper?" he asked, holding a large wooden pepper mill in both hands.

"None for me," Dillon said.

"Madame?"

"Just a bit," Ann said as he cranked the thing two or three times.

"Are we still working on the onion broth?"

"No, you can take it, please."

"Very well. Enjoy," he said, picking up the barely touched bowl along with Dillon's empty salad plate and then disappearing.

"I believe you were talking about compartmentalizing," Dillon said, grabbing his fork, attacking his dinner and not really meaning his statement to come out in that particular tone.

Apparently she was more than up to the challenge. "Jack, look, I get it. Okay? You have to leave tomorrow. I know, *it's your job.*" She said the last three words in a sing-song sort of tone that didn't do anything to improve the atmosphere. "I just wish you weren't leaving, that's all. Okay? Sorry if I told you the way I feel. Can we just leave it at that and not go any further? Obviously you're not in the mood to discuss it right now," she said, then picked up her fork and stabbed it into the duck breast, almost cracking the plate in the process.

"Hey, I wish I didn't have to leave tomorrow too. But I do, you're right, it is my job, and just like you, I take it seriously."

She looked at him and smiled, but it was a sad smile. She reached a hand across the table. He put his hand out and she squeezed it, then smiled another sad smile and said, "I think you're one of those people who always likes to get the last word in."

"No I don't."

The rest of the meal went relatively smooth, at least on the surface. But it was obvious the brief conversation remained in the back of both of their minds. They worked through the main course and their dessert with some occasional conversation, but the air had been let out of the balloon of excitement they had initially arrived in.

By the end of the meal they were both anxious to get the bill. Dillon kept looking for the server. Finally Ann spotted him and waved him over. Once paid, they strolled outside and he gave her a kiss in front of the place. The kiss seemed electric, and he thought, or rather hoped, that maybe they were back on track, but just as he began to pull her closer she stepped back.

"Probably better that we don't, you know. Early start tomorrow and all that. I'll see you in front of the Joy at eight. Don't be late," she said, and flashed a quick smile. Then she turned and hurried to a taxi waiting at the curb. Dillon just stood there and watched as she

126

climbed in, and a moment later the taxi drove out of sight.

Chapter Twenty

He started to walk back to the hotel, wondering about Ann. Would he ever see her again after tomorrow? Would he even see her tomorrow, or would she call in sick or ask for a last minute replacement or simply not show? Did he even want to see her? Of course the answer to that last question was a resounding yes.

It was a clear night, no clouds, the temperature was cooling down, and the foot traffic had thinned out considerably from what it had been just a couple of hours earlier. He could see the Gresham Hotel from where he stood. He was just across the street from the restaurant in front of a small park called the "Garden of Remembrance."

It was a memorial garden, *"Dedicated to all those who gave their lives in the cause of Irish Freedom."* They weren't kidding, the memorial listed uprisings beginning all the way back to 1798. The gates were locked at this late hour, but Dillon could see a sculpture at the far end of the park. He Googled it using his cellphone. It was a sculpture of the Children of Lir, symbolizing rebirth and resurrection. The sculpture had been added to the park almost a half-century ago in 1971. He'd have to use that fact tomorrow on Ann.

There was a large tree just outside the park wall with a half-dozen people sitting under it. They were passing around a bottle in a paper bag, four men and two women. Everyone took a swallow, then passed the bottle on to the next one. The bottle never, ever really stopped moving. Dillon could only imagine what brand of top shelf alcohol it contained.

"Two euros if you want to join us," one of them called out to Dillon as he walked past. A couple of the others laughed. One of the women grinned, exposing missing front teeth.

"Thanks, but no thanks," he said.

"Oh, a Yank. Better make that three euros," the voice said, and they all laughed again, only this time a little louder. Dillon gave a quick, friendly wave, but didn't look back and kept moving.

He stopped in the hotel bar to try and think over a glass of whiskey, wondering in the process if he really differed that much from the group passing the bottle around under a tree. Same thing, alcohol, although this was a much different atmosphere, theoretically a much better quality drink, and then there was the fact that he didn't have to share his glass with anyone.

"Jameson, on the rocks," Dillon said as the bartender stepped in front of him. The bar was almost empty. There were two older couples seated at a table in the far corner, laughing and talking. The men pointed fingers back and forth, and then all four of them would laugh at whatever the joke had been. Dillon suddenly envied them, yearned for the companionship and just now wished that Ann was here with him.

The bartender set his drink down in front of him and Dillon showed him the card that served as his room key so he could put the drink on his tab. He took a sip and glanced around the room. Two guys were chatting quietly at a far table. Young, maybe mid-twenties, certainly not older than thirty. They both gave a casual glance in his direction, held his gaze for a brief moment, then continued with their conversation. They were fit-looking and he guessed they either worked out regularly or were employed in something along the lines of construction or maybe farming. He'd either missed them before, when he first came in, or they'd just arrived.

Two middle-aged, heavyset women with half-finished glasses of red wine resting on the table in front of them stared out at some distant wall. They were seated side by side on a couch, although neither seemed to have ever said anything to the other. They appeared oblivious to one another, and for that matter everything else. He watched them for a long moment as they continued to stare, both of them looking unhappy. Not unhappy for the moment, but long-term unhappy, say for the past forty years, and more than willing to project that unhappiness to whomever ventured near. He had a sudden cruel thought about why there wasn't anyone with them.

He slowly finished his drink over the course of the next half-hour, then walked out to the main lobby and the front desk. The walls were white marble, at this hour the lobby was virtually empty and Dillon's footsteps seemed to echo as he approached the lone man standing behind the desk dressed in a grey suit and red tie, smiling politely.

"I'd like a wake-up call for tomorrow morning at six-thirty," Dillon said.

"Certainly, sir," he said. "May I have your room number, please?"

Dillon gave him the room number.

The man typed in the information on the computer, then nodded and said, "Very well, six-thirty it is then. You have a pleasant rest of the evening, Mr. Dillon."

He turned and almost ran into a muscular-looking young man standing directly behind him. He looked vaguely familiar, but it took a long moment before Dillon realized he was one of the two guys that had been quietly chatting in the bar.

"Oh, excuse me, sorry if I startled you," he said, then sort of side-stepped Dillon, and approached the man at the front desk. "I'd like to see if a package may have been delivered to the desk sometime today..." He had an accent, definitely not Irish, not German or French either, maybe Polish or eastern European.

Dillon took the elevator up to his floor and walked down the hallway toward his room. The hallway was painted a very light grey color, and at this hour on a Saturday night there didn't seem to be so much as a peep coming from any of the rooms. He half-wondered if he was the only person on the floor.

The light was on just inside his door. The sheets had been straightened and neatly turned down on the bed. A small white porcelain plate sat on the bedside table, holding two small, foil-wrapped "After Eight" mints. If he tried he could still pick up just the slightest hint of Ann's perfume from the pillow and the sheets. The pink bag with the "Ann Summers" in white letters along with her battery-operated toy lay on the upholstered bench at the foot of the bed. For a brief moment he half-wondered what the staff person would have thought, then decided they probably saw crazier things every day. He hurriedly undressed, climbed into the bed, closed his eyes and pretended Ann was still there.

Chapter Twenty-One

"That was him, the American. Dillon is his name. Some sort of cop. He's the one bringing Ackermann back to the States," Borya said. The two of them were in the back of the taxi just pulling away from the Gresham Hotel. They were speaking Russian.

"You're sure?" Yegor asked. He was blonde, with hair closely cropped along the sides and neatly combed over on top. He was anything but intimidating. At a mere hundred and fifty-five pounds, with just the hint of a sparse mustache that had already taken close to six weeks to grow to its current anemic state, he looked like that polite kid from just down the block. One would peg him for a student rather than an unemployed illegal hoping to make it big in criminal enterprise. "You're certain it was him?"

"No doubt. I heard him speak, definitely American, and then the man behind the desk called him Mr. Dillon. Bazanov's information is correct. I knew it would be."

"And tell me again why we just don't knock on the door to his room and then kill him when he opens the door?"

"Because he's not the target, the banker Ackermann is. This Dillon will just be additional damage," Borya said.

"I think you mean collateral damage," Yegor replied.

"Yes, that too."

The driver glanced in his rearview mirror and thought, *Fecking foreigners*. He made a left turn and took the long way to their destination up in the Finglas section of Dublin. If he had to listen to their gibberish they were damn well going to pay for it.

Twenty-five minutes later the taxi pulled to the curb in front of a small, one-bedroom flat. With the exception of the red door and a bicycle chained to the iron stair rail, the flat was identical to all the other units on the street. The driver reached across the front seat and pushed a button on his meter, then looked at his two passengers in the rearview mirror staring at the meter. "That will be thirty-eight euros, gentlemen. Do you need a receipt?"

The dark-haired one said something in his foreign gibberish, then pulled thirty-five euros out of his wallet and half-threw them into the front seat before he growled something to his friend. The friend responded in a tone that suggested he disagreed, then took three euro coins from a front pocket and handed them to

134

the driver. They climbed out of the taxi, slammed the door closed and headed toward the small flat.

The taxi man lowered his window and called, "No tip?" then laughed and sped off just as the two of them gave him the finger. He tooted his horn a couple of times as he pulled around the corner and disappeared out of sight.

At best the flat was compact. The red front door opened into a very small sitting room barely large enough to hold the worn couch, a wooden chair, and a sixty-inch flat screen TV Borya had "liberated" from a home over on the south side of Dublin not two weeks earlier. There being no central heating, a small, coal-burning fireplace was positioned just a foot or two feet away from the end of the couch. Fortunately, at this time of year no heat was needed.

They briefly talked, the two of them, about how they intended to carry out the operation tomorrow morning. From there they shared plans of what they'd do with the payment and where they'd live now that they were about to move up in the organization, Borya thinking some sort of mansion down in the Dublin 4 area. Yegor thought he would maybe acquire three or four women and just move from one to the other, never paying rent and spending no more than a week at a time with any of them. "That will just make them want me that much more."

A little after two they heard squeaking brakes out front. Borya, seated on the couch, lifted the bed sheet that hung over the front window and watched the lights turn off on the white van that had just pulled up in front of the flat. "Finally he's here." There was a knock on the door a moment after that.

Borya opened the door and growled in Russian at the young man standing outside on the front stoop. "Where in the hell have you been, Grigory? We expected you at least an hour ago."

He was heavier that Yegor, but not by much, with a shaved head. At least he could grow a proper mustache, and he stepped into the room, shaking his head. "Tell me about it. My stupid brother promised to be home by ten. Then guess who he picked up?"

"Who?" asked Yegor.

Grigory looked at Borya. "A guess? Who do you think? Come on, the two of you, guess."

Both Borya and Yegor shook their heads. Grigory nodded and laughed. "Darya," he said, and stood there smiling with his arms folded across his chest, nodding, looking like the cat that had swallowed the canary.

"You mean it? Darya? Really?" asked Yegor. He'd sat up on the couch and half shouted her name.

Grigory smiled and nodded.

"He's lucky to even be alive," said Borya.

"You don't know the half of it," Grigory said, then proceeded to provide them with the intimate details. It was close to a half-hour later before he had finished. Once he'd stopped talking all three sat in complete silence, lost in their own thoughts and Darya dreams for a long moment.

"She's going to be my first stop, once we complete tomorrow and get paid," Yegor said.

"I have to have the van back to my father's garage by tomorrow afternoon," Grigory announced. "Tell us how this will work...."

"Very simply," Borya said, then stood and waved Yegor off the couch. He got down on his hands and knees and pulled out a grey, moth-eaten, woolen blanket from beneath the worn couch. He looked up at his two accomplices, now holding their breath, then smiled and pulled back the folds of the blanket. Two automatic weapons lay on the blanket, black, cold-looking AK-74s with dark-brown plastic magazines lying next to them. A small pistol, with the loaded clip next to it, lay between the plastic, thirty-round magazines.

"Is that a Marakov?" Grigory asked, pointing at the small, black pistol.

"Yes. Not to worry, with all this we won't have any problems," Borya chuckled. "By the way, they'll all be unarmed."

Chapter Twenty-Two

Dillon slept fitfully and woke well before his wake-up call. He'd had nightmares off and on over the course of the night. Neither the wine with dinner nor the whiskey nightcap had seemed to help him sleep. He wondered if it was something he'd eaten, maybe the wood pigeon terrine. He couldn't quite remember what the dreams had been about, only that he kept waking with a start. He was tired, but didn't want to go back to sleep. He showered, shaved and got dressed, then sat in the straight-backed chair, waiting and thinking, trying to remember what the dreams had been about, until the wake-up call came through.

After he hung up the phone he strapped on his ankle holster with his .38, and snapped a second holster holding his Glock onto his belt just at the small of his back. He pulled his suit coat on, slung the strap of his computer bag over his shoulder, and wheeled his suitcase down to the lobby.

He was checked out of his room twenty minutes before the dining room opened. He sat on a couch in the quiet lobby and casually paged through a copy of the Sunday Independent newspaper. The headline news seemed just as bleak as the papers at home, and in short order he ended up sitting and staring at nothing for the next fifteen minutes until the dining room opened, reminding himself he was not like the two middle-aged women he'd seen the night before.

He was the first one in the dining room, in fact the only one at this hour on a Sunday morning. He took a table next to a window, set his suitcase next to the chair opposite him, laid the computer bag on top of the suitcase and sat down. He glanced around the dining room with all the tables set, silverware, glasses, white porcelain cups and plates all neatly arranged and no one but him in the dining room. Peace and quiet.

After last night's four-course meal he wasn't really that hungry, and he began to think about Ann. When it came time to order he ended up just ordering a cup of coffee, and then sat there staring into the coffee cup. He had a second cup of coffee, drank it down in about two minutes, then left five euros on the table and left.

He grabbed a taxi a few minutes before seven-thirty and was at the front gate of Mountjoy Prison five minutes later. The taxi man gave Dillon a long look once he climbed out of the taxi, apparently trying to figure him

139

out as he stood there in front of the main entrance dressed in a suit and tie with a suitcase and a computer bag. Ever the professional, the taxi man never said anything and eventually drove off shaking his head, Dillon becoming just another story crying for embellishment.

While Dillon waited he had the feeling he was being watched, then he caught sight of the cameras mounted on the prison wall above the massive blue timber door. For half a second he thought, *Wouldn't it be funny to moon whoever is watching, or maybe just look up and give them the finger*. Thankfully, common sense prevailed.

He probably checked his watch a half-dozen times over the next thirty minutes. He watched a woman through a second-floor window apply make-up for five or ten minutes before she pulled a shirt on over her head. Unfortunately, she never gave him the benefit of turning around, so things were left to his imagination.

A couple of young boys he pegged at about ten years old expertly dribbled a soccer ball back and forth as they headed down the street. They were dressed in uniforms, white shorts, blue jerseys and matching stockings, yelling and joking as they passed by, oblivious to him and obviously focused on the game in their near future.

A few minutes later a young man passed by, and flashed a quick smile in Dillon's direction. Dillon pegged him for a student and said, "Hi, how's it going this morning?"

The guy looked the other way and seemed to pick up his pace. He was lean, with the sides of his head shaved, long blonde hair was neatly combed on top of his head. Dillon was just far enough away to not see the anemic mustache the guy had been trying to grow for the past six weeks and watched him pass from view as he disappeared around the corner.

Once out of sight, the young man looked over his shoulder, then took off running toward the white van waiting just down the next street.

Dillon parked his suitcase and computer bag next to the massive blue front gate and then began to walk back and forth along the cobblestone street, never veering more than twenty feet from his computer bag at any time. About every thirty seconds he checked his watch until he finally took it off and put it in his suit coat pocket.

A couple came out of one of the residential buildings down the street and walked toward Dillon. She was dressed in a nice-looking, somewhat conservative dress, and he was wearing a dark suit along with a starched white shirt and striped tie. They nodded as they passed by, then turned at the corner and headed for St. Joseph's church two blocks away.

A taxi came down the lane a few minutes later and Dillon had a moment of excitement thinking it might be Ann showing up early. The taxi drove past him, the driver giving him a strange look as he passed, then stopped at the end of the street. A moment later a woman climbed out of the back and headed into one of the residential buildings. She appeared to be dressed in the stunning, sexy outfit she'd worn the night before, and Dillon concluded that her evening must have been a success.

The taxi man took his time backing up, glancing at Dillon a number of times as the taxi inched back toward a trimmed hedge. He straightened his wheels out then slowly drove toward Dillon and pulled to a stop alongside him. He lowered his window no more than an inch, then tilted his head up so he could talk through the small opening.

"Is it a ride you're needing?"

"No, thanks, I'm fine."

"Waiting to go in then?" he asked, and gave a halfway nod toward Dillon's suitcase.

"What? Oh, no, no, just meeting some people in a few minutes. Thanks for checking all the same."

"Mmm-mmm," the taxi man said, not sounding all that sure he'd been told the truth. He examined Dillon for another long moment, then gave a sort of "tip of the hat" wave and drove off.

Chapter Twenty-Three

Just as he was about to give up hope, two vehicles turned the corner and drove down the short street. The time was just a few minutes after eight. The first vehicle was a standard sort of white sedan with the words "GARDA" in blue letters across the front of the hood. A fluorescent greenish-yellow strip about five inches wide ran along the side of the vehicle with the same "GARDA" in blue letters across the doors. Flashing lights were mounted on top of the vehicle, and he spotted Ann seated in the front passenger seat. The vehicle behind it, also white, looked like more of an SUV. "GARDA" was stenciled in blue letters across the front of the hood with the same fluorescent strip, and "GARDA" on the sides. Identical flashing lights were mounted on top of the SUV. Two men sat in the front of the SUV.

Dillon thought he recognized Paddy Daly, the guy from the airport the other day, sitting in the front passenger seat of the SUV. Both vehicles stopped at the same time and the passenger doors seemed to open simultaneously. Ann got out of the sedan, then leaned back in and said something to the driver. She was wearing her uniform and to Dillon's mind still appeared gorgeous. She flashed a quick smile in his direction, but didn't say anything, quickly turning the other way. She carried a small black briefcase in her right hand. Other than the quick smile she didn't really look at Dillon, instead she just sort of stood there and stared at the ground.

For a brief moment Dillon envisioned her on her back, in his hotel room, wearing a smile, that small gold crucifix, and running her fingernails across his chest. From her current stance and the fact she wouldn't even look at him it appeared that wasn't going to be happening anytime soon. He wondered if she was wearing that same gold crucifix this morning, then sort of shook his head in an effort to return to reality.

Paddy Daly slowly climbed out of the SUV. The driver's door on the SUV opened and a bulky sort of guy climbed out and stretched for a long moment. They were both dressed in the same uniform as Ann, dark blue trousers, light blue shirt with dark blue epaulets, but neither one looked anywhere near as inviting as Ann.

Daly reached into the vehicle, grabbed his hat, adjusted it onto his head and grinned. He quickly placed two fingers between the bridge of his nose and the black bill on the hat just to make sure it sat at the proper angle. Then he

144

waved and called in a booming voice, "Marshal Dildo. Nice of you to join us. You look like you've just been released from the Joy, or better yet, like you're about to sign in for an extended stay."

Dillon looked around expecting to see shades raised and drapes pulled back up and down the street. He waved back at Daly and called, "There you go, you can fool some of the people some of the time. I checked. Fortunately they somehow missed the cell they were supposed to have reserved for me."

"A bit of trouble come your way?" Daly asked, walking toward him. He nodded to indicate the slightly swollen and bruised eye, now more of a fading purple with tinges of light brown around the edges.

Dillon thanked God for the dozen or so ice packs Ann had forced him to use and then caught her biting her lower lip in his peripheral vision. He gave half a chuckle, then said to Daly, "Yeah, I ended up going a quick round with an ironing board in my room at the Gresham. The ironing board won. The thing must have been spring-loaded and flew off the wall a little bit faster than I expected. Now, well, you can see the result."

"God, but you're an absolute danger," Daly said as he stopped in front of Dillon, then casually glanced up and down the street. He held out his hand and they shook as he said, "We've phoned ahead. They've got your man waiting in a holding cell. Garda Dumphy has the paperwork. I think we'll put him in our vehicle, we can secure him better in the back seat. We'll head out to the airport with the flashers on. I can't see any point in stopping at a traffic light this time of day, let alone on a Sunday morning.

"We'll bring the two of you into a side entrance at terminal two. We've a guard stationed at the entrance as we speak. There's a secure room there to hold him in. You'll remain separated from the other passengers until the flight is ready to board. Your man will remain in our custody until you board the plane, at which time you become the man in charge. You two will be the first ones on the plane. With any luck the other passengers won't have the faintest idea of the situation. No point in unnecessary panic. I trust you've escorted prisoners on flights before?"

"Many times," Dillon said, about to add, "But always in the States," then decided against saying that last bit. After all, what possible difference would it make?

"So you know the drill?"

Dillon nodded and said, "We board before everyone. I've got a nylon windbreaker to cover the handcuffs. At almost seventy years of age, Ackermann is rated as a low-risk physically. That said, I'd like your team to do a physical search. I'll do the same before we board. He'll be the only prisoner on the flight. Our policy is he remains handcuffed throughout the flight and is escorted to and from the restroom should he need to use it. While in the restroom he's handcuffed to one of the grab bars bolted on the wall. We'll take up residence in the second to the last row. No alcohol before or during the flight. Since the flight is more than four hours long, a second security officer will be on board to serve as an escort. My understanding is your service is providing that second escort," Dillon said, and then suddenly wondered if he might be lucky enough to have that second escort be Ann.

"And you're looking right at him." Daly gave a broad smile and spread his hands out, palms up. "I was able to parlay the trip into two days in New York. God, the wife's given me a two-page shopping list. So, what say we get going? Once we take Ackermann into custody, I think we'll have you ride with Officers Dumphy and Reilly. You'll be just ahead of us in the sedan. You can toss your suitcase into the boot there. Bobby," he called to the driver standing next to the open driver's door on the sedan. "Unlock the boot for your man so he can toss his luggage in."

The driver reached in and pulled a lever on the floor. A moment later the trunk popped open a good foot.

Daly and the other officer headed toward the front gate. Once they had stepped away, Ann quickly approached and stepped alongside Dillon. She spoke in a low voice and seemed to be gazing at the massive stone wall. "So, you made it back to the hotel all right?"

"No, I went out and partied all night long. Barely made it back in time for a shower," Dillon said. She gave him a quick look of surprise. "Relax, just kidding. But I slept fitfully. I really did miss you. I understand, but just so you know, I didn't enjoy your absence."

"I know, but it really was for the best," she said. "I want to thank you for the most lovely weekend I've had in a very long time. Well, in fact, it feels like maybe since forever. It's been a while since I really laughed like that and enjoyed someone's company."

"Me too. Thanks, Ann. I really mean it, and I'm not just talking about the late night."

"Or yesterday afternoon." She smiled. "Come on, lets get that suitcase in the boot."

He tossed his suitcase and computer bag in the trunk, closed it and glanced around to see where everyone was before he spoke. Then he quietly said, "Would I be too forward if I told you I'd really like to see you again? I'd like to come back sometime, that is, if you think you could stand me for a few days."

She looked up at him, and he could see her eyes were starting to tear. "Better get in the car, once they come out of the gate they don't like to wait around," she sniffled. "You can take the backseat and stretch out a bit. Probably be more comfortable for you, you've got a long flight ahead of you and you'll be riding with Paddy. No telling what he'll be up to."

"Just think about what I said. I really meant it." He nodded, then took hold of her hand and squeezed it. She gave a quick glance toward the front of the car to see if Bobby Reilly, the driver, was watching. He seemed focused on the gate, waiting for Ackerman to come out.

She squeezed his hand, then sort of turned it into more of a professional handshake before she hurried back toward the front passenger seat. She pulled open the rear door for Dillon as she went and said, "Go on now, you better get yourself in."

Daly and his driver walked back out of the gate a few minutes later. They gave a cautious look around before they nodded, and suddenly Ackermann stepped out behind them.

He appeared a lot different than the black and white photo Dillon had studied, but the photo was probably a good ten years old. He looked older, by a good twenty years, and substantially leaner, although that may have had something to do with a diet of prison food for the past three months instead of dining at the finest restaurants like he had for the previous ten years. His face appeared very drawn and pale with a long beak of a nose and thin lips. There appeared to be a bruise on the bridge of his nose, perhaps from an assault, although no one had mentioned anything about an assault to Dillon. His eyes, as he drew closer, seemed a flat, lifeless brown, and his grey hair was short and thin and appeared wispy on top.

He walked with a slight limp, although that may have been more a function of the shackles around his ankles. The grey suit he wore appeared to be expensive and, at this point, ill-fitting. His starched white shirt, buttoned all the way to the top although he wasn't wearing a tie, was too large around the collar, but again that may have been a function of weight loss due to his incarceration over the past ninety days.

He somehow reminded Dillon of an old guy you might see in the local grocery store, pondering the pricing on packages of pasta, debating the possibilities of saving a penny or two and in no particular rush because he had all day to do absolutely nothing.

They made a bee-line toward the SUV, five of them, Paddy Daly and the driver in front of Ackermann and two prison guards bringing up the rear. The guards appeared to be unarmed and Dillon wondered if Paddy would be armed on the plane. Ackermann seemed to move slowly, perhaps more of an age thing combined with the shackles than any sort of injury or intentional delay. After just a few steps and a word from one of the prison guards behind them, Daly had to turn and stop for a moment until Ackermann caught up, then proceed at a much slower pace.

The driver of the SUV hurried ahead and opened the rear door of the vehicle for Ackermann as Daly and the guards glanced in all directions. Ackermann gave a slight groan as he turned round and then settled into the backseat. His feet remained on the street and the driver had to reach down, grab the shackle chain and help lift Ackermann's feet into the backseat. The driver then attached a heavy cable running up from the floor of the SUV to Ackermann's handcuffs.

One of the guards leaned into the open rear door and appeared to give Ackermann a goodbye or wish him a pleasant flight or something just before he closed the rear car door. Daly and the driver gave a final look around then climbed into the front seat. The two guards gave another cautious look around before they both stepped back and gave a nod to the driver indicating they were good to go.

Bobby Reilly turned the sedan's flashers on and they pulled away from the curb and made a U-turn in the middle of the street. They moved ahead fifteen or twenty feet and Bobby held up for half a moment, watching in his side mirror. The flashers on the SUV suddenly lit up. They made the U-turn and pulled in behind the sedan. Once the headlights flashed on the SUV, they headed off down the street in the direction of the airport.

The traffic was almost nonexistent at this hour on a Sunday morning. They slowed at the first stop light just long enough to check for oncoming traffic as the light suddenly flashed green and they continued on their way. They weren't so much speeding as they were traveling at a normal pace. They passed a half-dozen cars that had spotted the flashing lights and pulled over to the side of the road during the course of their fifteen-minute journey. Traffic remained light all the way to the airport and the traffic lights immediately changed as they approached so they never had to stop even once.

Chapter Twenty-Four

No one spoke in the sedan for five or six minutes until Ann turned round in the front seat and flashed a wry smile at Dillon seated in back. "So, Marshal Dillon, I hope you enjoyed your stay in Dublin. Did you find it pleasant?" Her eyes seemed to suddenly twinkle and she raised her eyebrows in a manner that suggested a lot more.

"Yes, very nice."

"Do anything fun?"

"Yes, I took a bus tour of the city, went to the Guinness brewery, visited the art museum, toured the Temple Bar district. I saw a number of very interesting sights. I visited some churches and over the course of the weekend spent a good deal of time on my knees," Dillon said.

She suddenly blushed and got a surprised look on her face. Bobby the driver shot Dillon a brief look in the rearview mirror, cleared his throat, but didn't say anything. Once Dillon was sure he had refocused on the road he raised his eyebrows back at Ann.

"Yes, well I'm sure you enjoyed that, the church visits. Pity you weren't able to stay a bit longer and see some more of the sights. Always something of interest, some new experience," she said.

"I hope to be able to do a lot more of that next time. This certainly won't be my last trip over, I promise you that. I'm definitely planning to come back to Dublin again."

"Well, let's hope it's sooner rather than later. We'd love to see you again," she said, then turned round and faced the front. Occasionally she looked out the side window and rubbed her eyes, brushing a slight tear away and hoping Bobby Reilly didn't catch on. As they approached the signs for Dublin Airport she reached for some Kleenex on the console and blew her nose, then dabbed at her eyes.

"Bit of cold, Ann? You seem to be having the sniffles all of a sudden," Bobby said.

"No, no, nothing of the sort. It's just not very often I'm out of bed this hour on a Sunday."

"Well, whatever it is, don't be giving it to the likes of me," he said and laughed. He quickly checked his side mirror, then put on his blinker and pulled into the left-turn lane. He waited for just half a moment, then followed the signs directing them to terminal two.

* * *

"I think that's probably them making the turn now. The ones with the flashing lights coming this way," Borya said. He sat in the passenger seat.

"Really? God, I never would have known. Good thing you said something or we might have missed them," Grigory scoffed, then turned the key in the ignition and waited for the Garda vehicles to pass.

"About time," Yegor said from the back of the van.

They had been parked alongside the road to the airport for the past fifteen minutes, just one of three vehicles. Grigory had backed into a small paved area where people without anything to do parked and watched planes take off and land. He'd backed in at the far end of the area, far away from the other two vehicles. The road ran parallel to one of the major runways. The runway was separated from the rest of the world by a ten-foot-high cyclone fence topped with six strands of barbed wire.

A moment later the Garda vehicles with their flashing lights drove past at a moderate speed, and Grigory calmly pulled onto the road and followed behind them. On the far side of the cyclone fence, an airport security vehicle slowly passed by, heading in the opposite direction. Not for the first time, Borya checked the safety on his weapon clicking it on and then off again.

154

* * *

"We'll be going into the back side of the building. Up ahead where that gate is, that's where you turn. We've parking arranged, so we can avoid everyone. Once we get inside we've the private room and they'll send US Customs Agents down to clear Dillon, Ackermann and Paddy through customs while we wait," Ann said directing Bobby where to go.

He shot her a quick look. "Amazingly, I was at the exact same briefing. But I think I might know a shortcut," he joked. "If I just drive down the runway I figure we can get them on the plane one hell of a lot faster. Sound okay to you, Miss Bossy?"

Ann shot him a wide-eyed look of surprise, or maybe it was just fear, it was hard to tell.

"Would you ever relax, Ann? I'm just pulling your leg. What's got into you all of a sudden? It's like you're saying goodbye to a long lost love. Oh, wait a minute, yeah, of course. I just figured it out." He glanced in the rearview mirror and flashed a wide grin to Dillon. "Ann, don't tell me you've got a thing for this banking knacker, Ackermann? Are you feeling sorry for that banking bastard? Or is it all his supposed millions they've never been able to find? You got a thing for older criminals?"

"Ackermann? Me? You've got to be kidding. The man's old enough to be my grandfather. God, he wouldn't last two minutes, if he could

155

even perform to begin with. You'd better just pay attention to your driving, Bobby, or we'll end up getting clipped by one of those jumbo jets."

He put his blinker on, waited for a car to pass and mumbled, "Flashing lights, you plonker. Pay attention, damn it," then eased into the left-turn lane. The sound of the blinker was audible to Dillon in the backseat. He caught Bobby glancing into the rearview mirror again, only this time he was frowning. A moment later it dawned on Dillon that Bobby was checking something behind them and wasn't frowning at him.

He glanced over his shoulder, expecting to see the SUV with Paddy Daly and Ackermann behind them. Instead there was a shiny white van with magnetic signs on the doors that advertised Mullen Window Washing.

With the opposing traffic finally cleared, Bobby pulled the sedan across the oncoming lane, and drove up a short entrance ramp. A security guard in a white hard hat, a fluorescent green vest and carrying a clipboard signaled them to stop by raising his hand as he approached the driver's window. He had a radio device attached to his shoulder.

Bobby lowered the window and handed him some sort of form. "Prisoner repatriation. Flight info is on there. Delta Airlines, eleven o'clock, New York, JFK Airport in the States."

"Been waiting for you to finally show up," the guard said, then bent down to look in the car. He nodded at Ann like he knew her and proceeded to move his lips, counting the three of them. "It's been nice and quiet, no one who shouldn't be here."

"The other two and the prisoner are in the SUV behind this gobshite in the window-cleaning van that squeezed between us," Bobby said, and glanced again in the rearview mirror. "Stupid bastard."

The security guard glanced at the white van behind them and shook his head. "Eejit's eager to get the job done, I guess. 'Gobshite' doesn't even begin to cover it. I'll deal with the likes of him in just a moment. Okay, you know where to go. Follow the markings directing you to...."

"To holding unit C," Bobby said. "I was at the same briefing." He shot a quick glance at Ann, then waited while the guard wrote his initials on the paperwork and handed it back to him. Once finished the guard waved them ahead, then halted the white van that had pulled in between them and the SUV. He moved his hand in a circular sort of motion, indicating to the driver that he should roll down his window.

"Bollocks. Just what the hell part of flashing lights on two vehicles don't you understand?"

Grigory took his time lowering the window and smiled. Then in very broken English he said, "I clean windows." Borya looked straight ahead and clutched his weapon along his side.

"I'm aware of that much. I can read the damn sign on your door. But you're interfering in a police operation."

"Police?"

"Yes, you're in the way, now pull over here and I'll deal with you in a moment." The security guard stepped back and directed Grigory to pull over to the side with a wave of his hand so the SUV could pull in.

"You want me there?" Grigory asked and pointed off to the side.

"Yes, yes, for God's sake would you ever pay attention and move, damn you. You're in the way," he said, then frantically signaled again with his hand for Grigory to move the van.

Grigory smiled, nodded like he understood for the first time and pulled off to the side.

"All set," Borya said, climbing into the back of the van with Yegor, then grabbing the handle on the rear door.

"I'll make a quick turn and you can jump out. Leave the doors open so you can hop back in once you're finished."

"Let's go," Borya shouted a moment later as he and Yegor jumped out of the rear doors.

Chapter Twenty-Five

Bobby pulled ahead and around the corner of the terminal building, then drove parallel to the building for no more than fifty feet until they came to a half-dozen parking spaces up against the building. He turned the sedan so that it faced out toward the runway. Not too far off, a large airliner from Kuwait was just picking up speed as its engines roared and it headed down the runway. A moment later it took off up into the air. They watched it for a few more seconds and then Bobby backed up into one of four parking spaces next to a door. The parking spaces were marked by yellow lines and blue letters spelling out "GARDA."

"Here we go," he said, then turned the car off. Ann opened her door and climbed out. Bobby opened his door, then juggled the paperwork for a moment before tossing it onto the empty passenger seat. Ann opened Dillon's door, and he climbed out of the rear seat and quickly stepped close to her.

"Hey, you okay? I didn't mean to upset you. I'm sorry if I did," he said in a soft voice.

"Yeah, fine, just a momentary...." The sound cut her off in mid-sentence and she shot a questioning look at Dillon, then turned and took two or three steps before she shouted, "Oh no, oh no, Paddy," and started to run back the way they'd just come.

Dillon hoped it was just a car backfiring, while at the same time knowing he was absolutely wrong. The sudden chatter of more rounds being fired eliminated that fleeting thought. He took off after Ann. As he rounded the building he pulled the Glock from the small of his back.

In a nanosecond he registered the security guard in the fluorescent green vest lying face-down on the concrete, a growing pool of blood spread out from his body. Sheets of paper from his clipboard were caught in a light breeze and fluttered out across the tarmac toward the runway. His white hard hat was upside down on the pavement about five feet from his body. The back of the hard hat had been blown away.

The white window-washing van was in the process of making a sharp U-turn as the open rear doors on the van slammed back and forth. Two figures with black balaclavas pulled over their heads stood about ten feet apart, pouring rounds into the windshield and the side of the SUV.

AKs, Dillon thought.

The rear door where Ackermann had been sitting was already pockmarked with bullet holes and the window had completely disappeared. Ackermann was nowhere to be seen.

Ann was screaming, "Paddy, Paddy, Paddy," as she ran toward the SUV and the shooters.

Then things were suddenly moving in slow motion. The driver's door on the SUV opened and the driver half-twisted out, then seemed to float toward the ground. His body jerked as chunks of flesh were torn away. Blood splattered and misted along the side of the SUV. Both shooters continued to fire more rounds, and then what was left of the driver just hung there, upside down, with his face on the concrete and his legs still in the van.

At the sound of Ann screaming, the shooter on the right slowly turned and fired. Dillon heard something whiz past his ear. The shooter fired another round and Ann made a sort of grunting noise like she had just been punched in the stomach. She took a couple more steps, stumbled and seemed to be in the process of getting back on her feet when he fired again. She sort of groaned as she was knocked backward and dropped to the ground.

Dillon pointed the Glock and began firing. Things suddenly jerked back to moving at normal speed.

A misty cloud of blood erupted from the back of the shooter's head, and he crumpled on the spot. The second shooter turned and fired a burst at Dillon, but the white van suddenly came between them and the driver seemed to yell something.

Dillon fired at the van, saw a hole appear on the driver's door, pulled the trigger again, and another hole appeared. The driver sort of jumped and stared in his direction. Dillon raised the Glock slightly, fired twice more and the driver slumped against the steering wheel. As the van began to slowly roll forward, the second shooter suddenly reappeared.

Something whizzed past Dillon's ear and then it suddenly felt like someone kicked him solidly in his shoulder. He spun round and was knocked to the ground. He saw stars for a brief moment, then focused on the shooter walking toward him. He could see a pair of eyes glaring out of the balaclava as he aimed the AK at him.

Dillon raised the Glock, pulled the trigger, and heard "click."

* * *

Borya thought, It was all going so smoothly just a moment ago. The security guard had just finished asking Grigory, "What the hell part of flashing lights don't you understand?" He was pointing his hand off to the side as the SUV with the flashing lights had pulled up.

He and Yegor had quickly jumped out the rear doors of the van. Yegor fired a burst into the security guard while Borya began raking rounds back and forth across the windshield of the SUV. Then they heard the woman

162

screaming, and Yegor shot her. Now this whore's son just shot Yegor, stood there as he emptied his pistol into Borya's closest friend.

"I'll fucking kill you, you fucking pig," Borya screamed in Russian, and aimed at the wide-eyed man on the ground.

* * *

Someone yelled, "Bastard," behind Dillon, and the shooter refocused, aimed off to the side and fired a couple of rounds. Dillon tore the .38 from his ankle holster and started squeezing the trigger. The shooter jumped, shook his head like he'd just gotten sucker-punched, then took a step toward Dillon.

Dillon fired, and the shooter's weapon fell down to his side. Dillon fired again, and the weapon clattered onto the concrete as the shooter took a couple more clumsy, staggering steps toward Dillon. He kept pulling the trigger as the shooter twitched and staggered another step or two, then dropped to the ground and didn't move.

Dillon glanced around for anyone else moving, then suddenly became aware of the sound of a jet landing out on the runway. He looked over at Ann lying on her back on the concrete. One knee was halfway raised. Blood had soaked her shirt and was pooling on the concrete alongside her.

He tried to get to his feet, fell, and then, still holding the .38, crawled over to her on all fours. She looked glassy-eyed and blood was spouting from her upper chest. He placed a hand over her chest wound and pressed hard, but her blood just keep flowing and quickly coated both his hands.

"You're okay, Ann. You're going to be okay," he said, maybe trying just as hard to convince himself.

He heard someone from somewhere shouting, "Ann! Ann! Help! Someone help, damn it! Ann! Medic! Medic!" but never realized it was him doing the shouting.

Chapter Twenty-Six

The beep was regular, steady, nothing like an alarm clock although it did wake him. He lay there with his eyes closed for a while, attempting to do some mental accounting. He wiggled his toes first, one foot at a time. That seemed to work, so he moved the right and then the left foot. He moved his thighs and his ass. Everything seemed okay so far. He flared his nose, licked his lips, then wiggled his fingers. So far so good, except the left hand was awfully stiff and hurt like a bitch, still he was pretty sure it was still there. He was able to slowly move his head from left to right, and he tried to recall how in the hell he ended up wherever he was.

He remembered sitting in the back seat of the sedan, Ann turning to ask him what he'd done the night before and smiling. Bobby the driver told the security guard in the fluorescent green vest that a gobshite had pulled in behind them. Then it all seemed to get hazy and mixed up. Nothing seemed to make sense and he just had a lot of noise in his head, like a runway with a jet landing.

The airport.

He opened his eyes and stared up at an off-white ceiling. It looked higher than a normal room, there was no light fixture in the middle of the ceiling, and the deep seam running down the center suggested two panels of prestressed concrete.

He glanced left and right, and his first thought was that he had ended up in someone's bathtub. There was a white curtain draped all around him, and he gradually realized he was in a bed, although he couldn't remember whose house. At almost the same instant it dawned on him he was lying in a hospital bed, and the beeping he heard was coming from the stack of blinking monitors arranged behind him.

He lay there for a long while, trying to collect his thoughts and put things back in order. A fragmented picture slowly began to come together, and he suddenly remembered crawling toward Ann. The shock hit him like 1200 volts from a Taser as he recalled the image of her bleeding chest wound and not being able to stop it. He raised his hands and looked, but they were clean, and looked to have been freshly washed, although his left hand was wrapped in gauze, lots of gauze. The monitor screeching in his ear snapped him back to reality, and a moment later a hand reached in and yanked the curtain back.

"Oh, Marshal Dillon, are you okay? You gave us a bit of a fright there. We had a warning go off out at the nurses station. So you're coming around now, good. That's very good. How are you feeling, sir? How is that shoulder? Any discomfort?"

He didn't know if she was a doctor or a nurse, not that it really made any difference. She was slightly heavy, had shortish blonde hair, and she was wearing blue hospital scrubs with a stethoscope around her neck.

She moved swiftly along the side of his bed, checked a couple of monitors and flicked some sort of switch that stopped the infernal beeping. She grabbed the IV tube that he only noticed now for the first time, and seemed to adjust something. Then she placed the stethoscope on his chest, listened for a moment, moved it around and listened some more.

"How are you feeling, Marshal? How's that shoulder? Are you in any pain there?"

"Feels a bit stiff and hurts like a bastard. I can't move my fingers all that well on the left hand, and when I do, they hurt like hell, too. Kind of hazy as to how I got here."

She nodded like this made perfect sense. "All that's to be expected. And the head?"

"My head? A bit of a headache, kind of like a light hangover only without the party and the beverages beforehand."

"Vision all right?"

"Yeah, I guess so, nothing blurry. I can see you okay and that far wall. Haven't looked out the window yet."

She smiled. "You've a bit of a slight concussion. Looks like your head tried to go a round with the concrete and the concrete got the better of you. They put some plates and screws in your left hand to help with the healing. You fractured your hand, all four fingers and the thumb, when you, umm, fell. The plates and screws will be removed in a few weeks' time. We're going to let that heal up of its own accord."

"What happened? I mean, I know I was shot. But how long have I been here? What about...."

"I'm afraid I really don't have answers to most of your questions. And even if I did, unfortunately I'm not authorized to tell you anything. I can tell you this, first of all you're a very lucky man. There is no heart or lung damage. Like I said, you fractured the fingers in your left hand, probably when you hit the ground, same with the concussion. You were wounded in the shoulder, but that appears to have been a clean shot. The round traveled straight through. No arterial or organ damage. You must have received a lot of prayers and you're in pretty good shape, so your recovery should be relatively fast. The good Lord has been watching over you. Now, I'm to alert my supervisor that you're back with us, and she will in turn contact your embassy along with An Garda Síochána. Both have been very interested in your recovery."

"What about Ann? She was with us. Ann Dumphy? Did she make it? Is she going to be…."

"I don't know anything about that. She is not in our care on this wing," she said, but looked away from him as she spoke, and Dillon had the dreadful feeling she knew all too well how Ann was. "Now, I'm sure the people at the American embassy and An Garda Síochána will be more than happy to answer all your questions. You just relax for a bit, let me contact my supervisor, and we'll put things in motion."

"Can you at least tell me what time it is?"

She smiled and glanced at her watch. "Yes, I can do that. It's five minutes after three."

"Sunday afternoon?"

"Sunday? Oh, no, sir, today is Tuesday." She suddenly got a look on her face suggesting she may have said too much. "I'll be back with some water and juice for you, and we'll see about something to eat after that. I think…."

"Can you at least…."

"No, I can't." She smiled. "Now not another word, sir, and that's an order." She smiled as she quickly pulled the curtain closed around the bed and hurried out of the room.

Chapter Twenty-Seven

"Believe me when I say this, Marshal. No one, and I mean absolutely no one, would be happier than me to see you out of Ireland and on your way back to the United States just as soon as humanly possible. Good Lord, at this point I would consider paying for the flight myself."

She was long, lean, and woefully lacking any apparent sense of humor, let alone a pleasant personality. When she spoke she clenched her jaw in such a way that only her lips moved as she exposed her bottom row of teeth and addressed him in her Ivy League accent. She spoke slowly and distinctly, leaving one with the impression she thought you incapable of understanding what she was saying. At no surprise, she was devoid of anything resembling a wedding or engagement ring.

Vivian Strauss, Dillon's apparent contact at the US Embassy in Dublin, had apparently drawn the short straw when it came to the individual before her, namely US Marshal Dillon. She let it be known in no uncertain terms that she had been *forced* to deal with the likes of him. She made no effort to hide her distaste with the task at hand and was now in the process of patiently updating him...sort of.

"The hospital staff is telling us a minimum of another twenty-four hours before they'll even consider releasing you. Now, they just happen to be the experts here, so let's just see if we can't follow their advice. Shall we? The US Marshals Service has been in touch with embassy staff and they're in the process of flying a representative over from Washington in an attempt to allay some major concerns that have been brought to our attention by the Irish government. I'm unable, at this juncture, to predict with any certainty a level of success in that particular undertaking, it's all rather complicated."

"What major concerns of the Irish government? Do you know who the Marshals Service is sending over? And why are they even sending someone over? Maybe if I...."

She gave a quick roll of her eyes, held her hand up like a traffic cop, ignored his questions and moved on. "Please stop. The *individual* from the Marshals Service will be arriving tomorrow morning. And no, before you ask again, I've no idea who it is they'll be sending. Whoever it is, I'm sure they would like nothing better than to answer all your questions in a timely manner upon their arrival, so let's just leave that particular task to them, shall we? Which means that until that time, all I can suggest is that you remain patient and wait." She flashed a disingenuous smile, rose to her feet with a groan, and began to collect a number of files that she'd placed on the tray table. She appeared even less appealing standing up than sitting.

"Why is the Marshals Service flying a representative over? That sort of thing is usually reserved for…."

"Really, Marshal? I can't believe you're serious. Are you? Just for starters, you violated a number of…." She paused and searched for the proper terminology. "You violated a number of long-standing international agreements. This may be a very small country, but they still have their rights."

"I violated a number of agreements? What in the hell are you talking about? I'm transporting a prisoner, an American citizen, when three men begin shooting at him and the other law enforcement officers. All I did…."

"International agreements," she interrupted in a tone that suggested Dillon was either very stupid, not paying attention, or both. "Just for the record, Marshal, I hasten to point out the small yet pertinent fact that you were armed. Armed with a weapon, Marshal, and on Irish soil. This isn't the south side of Chicago, or some dreadful bar you might like to frequent. This sovereign nation happens to take a rather dim view of…"

"Those bastards at the airport were shooting people. They had automatic weapons they were firing. Firing at people. People that I knew and was responsible for. I wonder if you might point out exactly what in the hell was I supposed to do? They fucking murdered...."

"With all due respect, Marshal, profanity is not the answer, and I would respectfully caution you regarding that unprofessional attitude. This is the European Union, after all, not some barroom shouting match."

"According to my standing orders I'm required to be armed while escorting the prisoner back to the States. A member of the Garda Síochána was going to act as the second person on the security staff while on the flight. We've made no secret about...."

"Yes, we're all quite aware of the fact. That does not, however, permit you to drive willy-nilly through the streets of Dublin, the capital of a friendly nation, one of our most esteemed international friends, a member in good standing of the European Union, with you armed to the teeth and apparently just looking for trouble."

"Armed to the teeth? You might want to think about pulling your head out of your...."

"Please, Marshal, I might caution you about saying anything untoward, let alone anything that could be used against you in a court of law, either at home or here. Now, if there is nothing else, I've a rather busy day, so I'll leave you to a speedy recovery and...."

"Can you at least tell me if Ann Dumphy is alive?"

"Umm, no, I can't tell you. Only because I have no idea and it is not on my list of required matters to discuss with you."

"What about Paddy Daly or Bobby Reilly? Do you know if they made it? Everything was happening so fast that I...."

"Sorry, no can do. I simply do not have that information and I most likely never will."

"Then why are you even here? All I want to know is...."

"Please believe me when I tell you that this meeting was nowhere near the top of my list for the day's activity. Now, you have my card should you need anything, although it might be best to call the embassy's general number, which is also on my card, and they'll be able to direct you to someone else."

"I really doubt you'll be hearing from me," Dillon said, picking up her card for a brief moment before discarding it on the tray table.

"Believe me, that would suit me just fine, Marshal," she said. Then her mood seemed to suddenly brighten. "With any luck I'm off to London this evening. I plan on taking advantage of the weakening pound sterling with this dreadful Brexit situation while I can."

She wrapped a silk scarf once around her long, thin neck, tossing the end over her right shoulder. "So very nice to meet you, Marshal," she said, not meaning a word. She smiled coldly, turned and then strode purposely out of the room. Dillon lay in his hospital bed, waiting for her to pop back in the room, laugh and tell him the act was all a joke, but she never reappeared.

Chapter Twenty-Eight

The television in his room wasn't working, or had purposely been turned off. He wasn't sure which. It seemed obvious he was being kept in the dark and he couldn't figure out why. About a half-hour after worthless Vivian Strauss sashayed out of the room, a nurse came in.

"Mr. Dillon, I just wanted to check in with you before I went off duty. I'm thinking you'll be released tomorrow morning sometime. At least I hope so. Oh, sorry, I didn't mean that the way it sounded. I meant it would be nice for you to be able to leave the hospital and return home. Is there anything you need before I go?"

"Can you find someone who can get this TV working? I'm going out of my mind just lying here twiddling my thumbs."

"I'm afraid not, sir. I've put a request in, but that usually means three or four days before they even get back to me. I'm sorry, but that's just the way it is at the moment."

Dillon shook his head in disbelief.

"If you don't mind," she said, then glanced over her shoulder to make sure no one was about to enter the room. "I wondered if I could trouble you for an autograph." She sort of shrugged and smiled at the last word, then held out a tablet of lined paper and a pen.

"An autograph? Why on earth do you want my autograph? Or are you just nuts?"

She smiled at that last statement and glanced over at the non-functioning TV. "Well, I suppose since you've no way of knowing, you're, well, you're kind of famous."

"Famous? Me? How does that work?"

"You saved Garda lives, shot three really bad Russian gangsters. I'd say that's not bad just for starters. There's a whole lot of people praying for your speedy recovery in this little country. The Garda have tried to keep everything quiet, we all know about the shootout, but it's a secret that you're recovering in this hospital."

"Saved lives? Who?"

"Why, well, umm, maybe I shouldn't have said anything. Please don't tell anyone, I could lose my job if they found out. We were warned not to talk with you. It just sort of slipped out."

"Can you tell me, was one of them Ann? Ann Dumphy?"

"I'm not supposed to say anything."

"Please, just tell me if Ann is alive?"

She gave a quick glance in the direction of the door, looked at Dillon for a brief moment, stared at her feet and shook her head. "No, I'm

177

sorry, but I can't say anything. I'd lose my job if I did, and besides, I really don't know. Honest. Everyone involved has been scattered around the city in different locations. I guess that's probably some sort of security measure. You know, for your own good and protection," she said, and then looked like she was about to hurry out of the room.

"Hey, wait a second, you want this autograph, don't you?" Dillon said. Then he wrote, "Thanks for taking such good care of me," in large letters across the page and signed his name below that.

"Oh, you are so sweet. Thank you. I'm going to frame this at home. Let me just see if I can't rustle up another dessert for you," she said, then almost ran out of the room.

Chapter Twenty-Nine

Dillon was alone in the hospital bed over the next hour, clenching his fists and wiggling his fingers. The initial stiffness he first felt had improved substantially, and the headache seemed to have completely subsided. He was in the process of wondering how far he could get if he climbed out of bed and just walked out of the hospital. That thought led to wondering where, exactly, his clothes were.

He was about to sneak out of the bed and look in the small closet when there was a knock on the door, and in walked an attractive young woman carrying what looked like a food tray. She was a nice-figured brunette, and wore what seemed to be the standard blue hospital scrubs with a stethoscope hanging from her neck.

His stomach growled in immediate response to the food.

"Oy, let's see if we can't do something about that. My name is Maureen. I'm on duty this evening. You need anything, you can press that button just there." She pointed to the railing along the side of the bed with a small device clipped to the side. "That'll call me, but it better be worth the effort. I'm minding a lot of patients," she said, then smiled. "You need anything, dear? How's the head feeling?"

"Headache is gone. Of course, that might just suggest I don't have a brain. What's for dinner?" he asked, and nodded at the food she'd set on the tray table and was just now wheeling in front of him.

"Let's just see. I'm sure nothing but the finest from our five-star hospital restaurant," she said, then laughed and lifted the cover resting over the plate. "I think that's chicken, well unless it's pork." She sort of wrinkled her nose. "Yeah, it's chicken, I think. Plus peas, I guess those are roast potatoes, looks like a piece of apple crumble for dessert, although it could be a slice of really old cake. I'd say you're sorted."

"I'd say I'm starving."

"Then have at it. Oh, and…." She glanced at the door, then drew closer and whispered, "There are two Garda outside, waiting to come in and talk to you. I told them to stay out until they hear from me. I can send them on their way if you'd like. It's no problem if you don't feel up to it. I'm not about to have the likes of them harassing any of my patients. Especially one of my favorite patients," she said and smiled.

"I bet you say that to everyone."

180

"Yeah, you're right, I do, so don't you go getting all high and mighty and taking on airs."

Cops outside. *And so it's about to begin*, thought Dillon, the interviews, although "interrogation" was probably more like it. He thought about telling her to send them away, then figured, What the hell? He needed something to do.

"Tell you what, if I can eat while they're in here giving me the third degree, feel free to send them in. If I get tired, I'll just push that button and you can run in here and kick them out."

"Works for me, Marshal. You sure? It's no problem for me to just tell them both to go feck off."

"Thanks, but no. I'm going to have to deal with it sooner or later, so I might as well get started."

"All right, just as long as you're sure," she said, and looked at him for some sign of assurance.

He shoveled a piece of chicken into his mouth and gave her a nod. "Yeah, go ahead and send them in."

"All right then. Brace yourself now. They'll be heading your way just as soon as I'm out your door. They get to be too much, you just press that button and I'll shoo them away for you." With that she turned on her heel and left.

The door hadn't completely closed before it was pushed back open and two guys wearing ties and coats walked in. They looked like cops. Even the smiles were cop smiles. They seemed nice enough, but you could tell the wheels were turning behind the smiles.

"Marshal Dillon." The smaller of the two sort of charged ahead with his hand extended. His tie had a loose knot and was pulled down enough to expose the top button of his shirt, which appeared to be undone. He was bald, shiny bald. Close-cropped grey hair ran around the sides of his head. He had bright blue eyes and a neatly trimmed grey mustache. He appeared solid in a brick pillar sort of way, and he moved closest to Dillon.

"James McCabe, Garda Síochána Special Detective unit. This is Peter Mahoney." He indicated the man behind him with the briefcase, who simply nodded and smiled. No doubt he carried all the interrogation forms in the briefcase.

Dillon held out his hand, and McCabe shook it. He didn't squeeze hard, but as Dillon grasped his hand he could tell it had the consistency of concrete.

"Nice to meet you."

"Believe me, it's my pleasure. I appreciate you letting us interrupt your evening." He glanced around the room and took in the bare surroundings. "You like it quiet? Can we turn on the telly for you or something?"

"Apparently it doesn't work. They said it would be three or four days before they can get someone to take a look at it."

"That sounds like pure shite. Check it, Pete."

Mahoney set the briefcase on the end of the bed, then walked over to the television mounted on the wall. He picked up a remote from a small table, pushed a button, and the screen immediately came to life.

"Seems they were able to suddenly get it fixed. Not that there's ever much worth watching," Mahoney said, then walked back to the bed and set the remote on the tray table next to Dillon's food.

"Please, don't let the likes of us slow you down. Go ahead and eat before that gets cold," McCabe said. "We won't take up much of your time. I'm sure you're exhausted. We just wanted to come in, pay our respects and thank you on behalf of the force."

"Thanks," Dillon said, and nodded. He gave a polite smile, placed another forkful of chicken in his mouth and chewed while he waited for the other shoe to drop.

"I don't know if you're aware of this, but you're going to be interviewed tomorrow. Apparently your Marshals Service has someone flying over this evening."

"The first I heard about any of this was earlier this afternoon. A representative from the American embassy informed me that someone would be coming over, but she was unable to tell me who it will be, or for that matter what the interview will be regarding."

McCabe nodded, and felt his early suspicions had just been confirmed. They were keeping the guy in the dark. He'd been unable to discover what this Dillon had done that had pissed off his superiors, and right now he didn't really care. The guy had saved Garda lives and turned a potential international disaster into a heroic stand. He thought for just half a second then made up his mind, fuck the man's superiors. It wasn't going to happen, not on McCabe's watch, at least not if he could do something about it.

"We plan to begin the interview as soon as the individual arrives. Someone from our team will meet them at the airport and escort them here, to the hospital. We'll try to have an individual in there with you at all times, for purposes of representation, make sure no one is crossing any boundaries unduly, but if they request privacy I'm sure you understand we may well have to oblige." With that he nodded at Mahoney, who turned the briefcase so that it faced himself and snapped the two locks open.

Nice way to start the interrogation, Dillon thought, and gave what must have looked like an absent look out the window. It was sunny outside with scattered clouds, the sort of day he normally would have called "nice" - except he was lying here in a hospital room, about to get the boom lowered on him. *Might as well bring it on*, he thought

"Marshal? Marshal Dillon?"

He took a deep breath, wished he was outside, or better yet back in the States. First there was Vivian Strauss from the embassy, and now these two guys, a regular one-two punch. *Just get it over with*, he thought and turned his attention back to McCabe.

"Marshal?"

"Sorry about that. I believe you mentioned you were about to discuss the interview."

"So, I hear they call you Dildo," McCabe said, and smiled.

"You want to just get to your questions?" Dillon said, then speared a potato slice with his fork and stuffed it into his mouth.

McCabe nodded at Mahoney, who opened the black leather briefcase. Dillon suddenly heard what sounded like velcro being pulled apart. A moment later Mahoney placed a fifth of Midleton Irish whiskey on the table. He made a show of arranging three small crystal glasses in a straight line, then took his time carefully opening the bottle.

"Doctor's orders." McCabe smiled as Mahoney began to pour a generous amount into each glass. Dillon watched as he leaned over to examine the glasses from the side, making sure an equal amount of whiskey was in each glass. When he'd convinced himself each glass held exactly the same amount he gave a nod. McCabe handed Dillon a glass. He and Mahoney each took a glass and clinked them in front of Dillon, then waited until he joined in.

"Sláinte," they said, and everyone took a sip. The Midleton went down wondrously smooth.

"It means 'health,'" McCabe said, then the two of them took a second sip.

Dillon nodded and followed suit.

"Where to begin?" McCabe said. "First of all, you should know our visit here is unofficial, should you mention this to anyone we'll simply deny it. We represent members of the force, all of the Garda Síochána actually, and we would like to thank you for your actions on Sunday morning."

"Thank, thank you," Dillon said, more than a little stunned.

"I can give you some information, again unofficially, and we'll deny ever talking to you should word get out. If you want to wait for the official version with the arrival of your representative tomorrow morning that's your decision, we'll simply finish our whiskey and we can part as friends. It's your choice, Marshal. Absolutely no pressure here, on our part. We'll abide by whatever you decide to do."

Dillon pondered that for a long moment. "So if you're here today, unofficially, I'm guessing there's some sort of a problem. Otherwise you wouldn't find it necessary to cover your trail."

"There is absolutely no problem with us, Marshal, believe me. No, I'm afraid the problem seems to be coming entirely from your side of the water. Tell me, does the name Assistant Chief Deputy August Dahlquist happen to mean anything to you?"

Dillon groaned inwardly. "God, he heads up our department. He's my boss actually, and not what you'd call a big fan of mine. Although as far as I know he's not a big fan of anyone, well, except himself. How is he involved in the airport incident?"

"He seems to be drawing a fine line with the fact that you were armed prior to boarding the aircraft. Technically, that's a violation of international agreements, although we can argue that should it actually become an issue. He's got some plonker in the Dáil, that's our government…."

"Like one of your houses of Congress," Mahoney chimed in, and then drained his glass.

McCabe gave him a quick glance, then continued, "He's got this knacker out there stirring the pot, suggesting you being armed was the reason for the gun-play in the first place. Absolutely ridiculous, but under our laws he's a right to be just as stupid as he wants."

"What? You've got to be kidding me. I wasn't even there. I mean, we were around the corner of the building when we first heard the shots. I just ran in that direction and…."

"Believe me, we are well aware of that fact. As a matter of fact the entire incident was caught on a security tape. Our point is that there's likely to be some trouble for you when you get home. Your man Dahlquist appears to be setting up a disciplinary meeting regarding regulations and international conventions. To put it bluntly, Marshal, your man is going to try and royally screw you up the arse," McCabe said, then drained his glass.

"Dahlquist, I should have guessed. No real surprise there. So, can I ask you something?"

"Sure."

"Ann Dumphy? Can you tell me anything? I've asked the others, the woman from the embassy, the nurses, but no one seems to know or at least they won't tell me anything."

McCabe set his glass down and nodded at Mahoney, who refilled the glass. He took a healthy sip, cleared his throat and looked Dillon in the eye. "She's alive. I can tell you that she was resuscitated twice, once in the ambulance on the way to the ER, and again on the operating table. She is currently in a medically induced coma. Here's our simple take on the situation, I think I can safely state everyone would have been killed were it not for you and the action you took."

"Thank God, she's okay. I, I guess I was afraid she wasn't going to make it. There was so damn much blood and I just, well, you know, I just hoped against the odds that…." Dillon's voice sort of cracked, and he quickly downed what remained in his glass, cleared his throat a couple of times to regain control, then set the empty glass on the table. Mahoney refilled the glass and McCabe handed it back to Dillon.

He took another sip, then sort of stared off in the distance.

"She's not exactly okay. As I said, a medically induced coma for the time being, but given the other option, she's damn lucky you were there. We all are. The shooters," McCabe went on. "As near as we can figure out, they are, or rather were, members of a Russian gang working here and on the continent. They are headed up by a gentleman by the name of Alexei Bazanov. We've been battling them for some time without much success. The incident on Sunday marked an extreme escalation on their part. Your actions in response actually amount to our biggest success thus far."

"Success? Humph, Dahlquist is going to nail my ass to the wall." Dillon shrugged, then took another sip. He knew Assistant Chief Deputy Dahlquist well enough to realize he'd do everything in his power to take full advantage of the opportunity to derail Dillon's career, if not have him dismissed from the service altogether. Didn't matter what they thought here, back home his career was going to be toast, burnt to a crisp toast, and there wasn't a damn thing he could do about it.

"Now, Marshal, you don't have to answer just now. In fact, it might be better if you didn't answer, and just slept on our idea, but I think we might be able to provide a way out for you, of sorts, at least provide another option for you rather than flying back to the United States and having to face a disciplinary situation or even a termination."

"Oh?"

"As I said, you don't have to answer, but hear me out. What if we could arrange some sort of liaison position for you here? You'd be stationed here in Ireland and working with us."

"Why would you do that?"

"Well, the soft reason is to pull your feet away from the fire back in the States. There's a strong sense that we owe you. But the real reason is strictly self-serving."

"Self-serving?"

"You killed three members of this gang. Nothing like that has ever happened to them before, at least not here in Ireland. It's why we've had two armed officers outside your door for the past three days. To be brutally honest, we'd like to offer you up."

"Offer me up?"

"We'd like to get these bastards to come out of the shadows and show themselves for once. As I said, the incident at the airport was a major escalation. I think at this stage it would be more than a little naive to hope they just crawl back under the rock they came out from."

"You mean set me out there as a big fat target, and then I can just hope you get to them before they get to me, that it? You sort of paint a bullseye on my back and I wait for them to react."

McCabe seemed to think about that for a moment, then said, "Yeah, I'd say that's pretty much it, in the proverbial nutshell. I won't lie to you, it would be a dangerous undertaking."

Dillon shook his head back and forth, then looked up at McCabe. "I don't even have to think about it. There is no way in hell I would miss the opportunity. Count me in."

"So you're on board? If we can put it together you'd be a part of the operation?"

"Most definitely."

McCabe nodded at Mahoney, who topped up Dillon's glass, then began to place the bottle back in the briefcase.

"Hey, wait a minute. Don't tell me you're not leaving the bottle? I was just getting used to it."

"You've got to be kidding. It's Midleton, for Lord's sake. You don't just leave this lying around for any bollocks to help themselves, no offense intended. Now, if you'll excuse us, we've got some things to get lined up before your man arrives tomorrow morning. It's been a true pleasure. And again, my personal thanks for your efforts," McCabe said.

Dillon drained his glass, then handed it to Mahoney, who dutifully returned it to the briefcase. They both shook his hands, and a moment later were out of the room.

Dillon thought about their conversation for a minute, wondered how McCabe's suggestion would go down with the powers that be in the Marshals Service then picked up the remote and started flipping through the channels.

Chapter Thirty

A different nurse was in the following morning, giving Dillon fresh pillows and attempting to help him to the bathroom. She was a petite Asian woman who stood no more than five feet even. Her silky black hair was cut about two inches above her shoulders. He guessed her age at late twenties, and her looks at ten out of ten. She was gorgeous and her name was Lin.

"Really, I think I can make it on my own," he said, grabbing the stand the IV bag was hanging from and thinking he'd just roll it toward the bathroom.

She ignored him, took his right arm in her right hand and wrapped her left arm around his waist, sort of snuggling next to him, at least, that was the way he looked at it. On second thought, as she pressed herself against him he decided he probably did need the help.

"Oh, yeah, now that you mention it, it's much easier with you next to me. Yeah, I can really use the help." Then figured she probably heard that on a daily basis and just ignored it.

"A razor, shave cream, toothpaste and toothbrush are in there next to the sink. I'll just wait for you to come out," she said ten steps later. She smiled and opened the bathroom door for him.

"I may be a while. You sure you don't want to join me? Be a shame if I had to call for help."

"Not a bother. I'll just wait out here."

It was a bigger pain than he expected having to shave while his left arm was in the sling. The fingers on his left hand were still stiff, and about the best he could say was that they didn't seem to hurt quite as much as the day before. The bruise on his face where he'd bounced off the concrete had developed a yellowish-green tint around the edges. His left eye still looked horribly bloodshot, but when he closed the right eye the vision in the left seemed okay. All in all, given the circumstances and the potential for disaster, he thought he looked pretty damned good.

When he opened the bathroom door fifteen minutes later and stepped out, Lin immediately jumped out of the visitor's chair. "Everything go all right? Any problems?"

"I think it went better than I have a right to expect. The good news is, as awful as I look, it ain't that bad."

"Well, we've a couple of different options for you. First of all, I guess someone from the American embassy here in Dublin and someone who just flew in from Washington will be meeting with you here at the hospital. An Inspector McCabe with the Special Detective Unit dropped off some clothes for you. A pair of trousers, and a shirt which I'm afraid...."

"I'm not too sure the shirt is going to work," Dillon said, and indicated his left arm in the sling.

She smiled and said, "Inspector McCabe was counting on that. I've been given some *unique* instructions on how to dress you," she said, and gave a sexy smile.

"Dress me?"

She nodded and flashed that sexy smile again.

Who was he to argue with hospital procedure? Helping him into the trousers went all too fast. He slipped his right arm into the shirt, pulled it up over his shoulders and then Lin produced a small pair of scissors and proceeded to cut the left sleeve off. She set the sleeve on the bed, then slit the shirt maybe six or eight inches along the seam.

"I'm not sure you had to do that?" he said, glancing at the sales tags from the shirt that were lying on the bed. It seemed like a shame to ruin the shirt for this meeting.

"Just following orders from your Inspector McCabe." She smiled, then gently slid his arm through the hole in the shirt. She draped the sling around his neck, then eased his arm into the sling. He might have grimaced once or twice, but it could have been a lot worse. She slipped a new pair of socks on his feet, then

194

opened the small closet and pulled out his shoes.

"What, no new shoes?"

"Afraid not, but then again you're going to be in a wheelchair so it's not like you'll need them."

"A wheelchair?"

"Orders."

"McCabe?"

She nodded. "You're going to be meeting with everyone in a conference room down on the third floor. They'll call me when I should bring you down. Now, one more thing," she said, then pulled a small brown bottle out of a pocket in her scrubs. She unscrewed the cap, then placed a length of gauze over the top of the bottle, shook it once, then moved the gauze slightly and repeated the process a number of times. The gauze eventually had a large red stain across it.

"What is that stuff?"

"Food coloring," she laughed.

"What?"

"Oh," she said as something in her pocket beeped and she pulled out a cell phone. "Hmm-mmm, looks like they're ready for you." She folded the stained gauze over a few times, then gently attached it to his shoulder with white tape. "Just a little window dressing to help the cause."

He looked down at his shoulder. The food-colored gauze made it look like fresh blood was seeping from the wound. "You're kidding?

This is going to work?" he said and looked at her.

She shrugged, smiled, and said, "Just following orders."

"Okay, I guess we'll just have to see."

"A little more positive thought couldn't hurt," she said, then stepped outside the room. She was back a minute or two later, pushing a wheelchair. "Okay, climb in," she said and half-laughed.

"Is that thing really necessary?"

"Of course. Look, everyone will think you're bleeding, and therefore you need this. Now, quit wasting time and hop in so I can take you down to that meeting."

Chapter Thirty-One

Once outside the room they were escorted down to the third floor by two burly-looking Garda who no one would dream of tangling with. The meeting was in a conference room in the rear of a series of offices.

Lin knocked, and then one of the Garda opened the door and she wheeled Dillon in. McCabe was sitting at a far corner of the table next to two other guys Dillon didn't recognize.

Vivian Strauss from the embassy stood in a far corner, looking just as awful as the day before, only this time in a long paisley skirt that hung down to her ankles and a limp silk blouse that did nothing to help her lack of figure. She wore large, hoop earrings that seemed to accentuate her long, thin neck.

"Thought you were headed to London?" Dillon said.

"Unfortunately not. I was informed this meeting takes precedence and I was forced to cancel the plans I'd made more than a month ago. Most upsetting, I can assure you," she said, sounding none too happy.

A guy in a pinstriped suit with close-cropped hair sitting near whiney Vivian had quickly stood and stepped forward as Dillon was wheeled in. He was lean, like a marathon runner, and for just stepping off an overnight flight he appeared clean-shaven in a freshly starched shirt and suit. He paused for a half-second, and focused on the blob of food coloring soaking into the gauze bandages on Dillon's shoulder.

"Marshal Dillon, Everett Adams. We'll try and keep this short for you." He looked over at Lin. "Should he even be out of bed? That wound looks rather wicked."

"I think he can stay for a short while, sir. He insisted on attending. I'll be here to keep an eye on him."

Everett Adams, Dillon knew of him only by reputation. He lived and died for the Service, supposedly did everything exactly by the book, and hadn't seen a lick of field work in at least twenty-five years. Disposing of a wayward ne'er-do-well like Dillon, regardless of circumstance, would be right up his alley, and Dillon immediately felt the few options he thought he'd had just a moment ago being tossed out the window.

He glanced around as Lin wheeled him to the far side of the large wooden table. It was the first conference room he'd been in that had an anatomically correct human skeleton hanging in the far corner. Everyone had notepads, files and stacks of forms spread out in front of them. Lin wheeled Dillon into the one open space at the table. Not so much as a pen rested on the completely clear area in front of him, and neither Vivian Strauss nor Everett Adams thought to offer him pen or paper.

McCabe took over the moment Lin stepped away from the wheelchair. He cleared his throat, then said, "Marshal, let me introduce myself." He paused for half a second and gave a momentary hard stare in the hope Dillon would catch on.

"My name is James McCabe. I'm with the Special Detective Unit of the Garda Síochána. I want to, first of all, thank you, for your actions at the Dublin Airport on Sunday morning. Your selfless action saved the lives of two of our officers, Ann Dumphy and Bobby Reilly." He glanced at Vivian Strauss and then Everett Adams as he said this, daring a comment. Strauss, suddenly busy writing on the pad of paper, frowned but never looked up. Adams, ever the professional, remained stoic. "As a force and a nation, we remain in your debt, sir. I can assure you, should you be in need of anything while here in Dublin, you need only to contact me."

Before Dillon could respond, Adams said, "Thank you for your kind words, Detective McCabe."

"Actually, it's Detective Chief Inspector," McCabe said with a sharp smile, maybe setting the tone for what was soon to follow.

Adams ignored that last barb, cleared his throat and began to deliver his prepared speech. "While we recognize the valor with which Marshal Dillon acted this past Sunday, and let me state here that, on behalf of the US Marshals Service, and the United States, I wish to extend our deepest condolences on the losses the Garda Síochána and your nation have experienced." He paused for a moment and bowed his head ever so slightly.

"That said, I have the unfortunate duty of dealing with the fact that Marshal Dillon was armed while traveling through the streets of your capital. This is contrary to international agreement, casts a disparaging shadow on the United States Marshals Service and, I'm afraid, places Marshal Dillon in direct violation of section...."

Vivian Strauss suddenly looked up from her scribbling, unable to contain herself any longer, and interrupted, "One simply has to wonder if the outcome may have been different were the Marshal not armed. Might cooler heads have prevailed? In his rush to behave in this wild west fashion, did he in fact escalate the situation, which then resulted in the violent outcome? It would seem to beg the question that if Marshal Dillon, instead of randomly shooting, had attempted to defuse the situation by negotiating...."

Adams flashed a quick look at her, and flared his eyes in a way that suggested he wasn't used to being interrupted, and certainly not by someone at her level.

"If you'll please excuse me," McCabe interrupted. "Last time we checked, Marshal Dillon was a US Marshal. Negotiating? You did state that you were with the embassy, didn't you? The American Embassy? As in the United States, the country that originally dispatched the Marshal to escort a convicted criminal back to the United States."

"Why yes, I...."

"Just checking. Perhaps I misunderstood, but I wasn't really sure exactly whose side you were on here."

"I can assure you I merely...."

"I can assure *you* we'd have two more Garda dead were it not for the individual you're attempting to crucify here. Have you even thought to view the security tapes before inserting your foot in your mouth?" McCabe suddenly grew red-faced and raised his voice. "For God's sake, our two officers were murdered. Shot down in cold blood, didn't stand a damn chance. Negotiate? For God's sake. I've got to face the two families of those officers in the next few days, explain to them why there's an empty place at the dinner table that will never be filled. It's only due to Marshal Dillon's swift reaction that I don't have four families to face. Play the damn tape, Noel," he said, and the man to the right of him picked up a remote control and pressed a red button.

The flat screen on the wall suddenly sprung to life and Adams and Strauss half-turned in their chairs to watch. It was a grainy black and white image, one of the security tapes from the airport. As the rear doors to the white van flew open the man with the white hard hat jerked a couple of times and fell to the ground. The two men wearing the balaclavas began firing into the SUV as the driver tumbled out the door and the window where Ackermann was seated just a moment ago exploded.

One of the shooters turned, aimed and fired just as Ann Dumphy came into view. A moment later the back of his head exploded and he crumpled to the ground. The second shooter turned and fired, and there was Dillon suddenly on the screen, spinning round and dropping to the ground.

"I think we've seen just about enough of this," Vivian Strauss half-shouted and then proceeded to cover her eyes.

McCabe nodded to the man next to him and the flat screen was suddenly turned off.

"I believe you had mentioned something about Marshal Dillon negotiating," McCabe said calmly. Then his face suddenly flushed and in a much more forceful tone he said, "Negotiate? I seem to be at a loss here. Perhaps with all your experience you might be so kind as to point out exactly where? When?"

"I merely suggested that things..." she said, still with her hands covering her face.

"Here's my negotiation. I can promise you that the moment this meeting is concluded I intend to make a full report through the proper channels as to the conduct the two of you are exhibiting here. Negotiate? Rather difficult making one's self heard when you've to yell over automatic weapons firing at you. Negotiate?" McCabe spit the word out and threw his pen on the tablet in front of him. "One of our officers, Paddy Daly, was shot nineteen times. Nineteen times. At what point, under those sorts of circumstances, does one begin to negotiate? Please, tell me, I'm all ears, I'd love to know."

"I was merely stating the fact that the international convention...."

"For God sake, your man is still bleeding in case you hadn't noticed. And the two of you intend to haul him back to Washington, where he'll be drawn and quartered by some political hack? Not on my watch. In fact, let me take it a step further and suggest to you that under the circumstances An Garda Síochána intend to extend an offer to Marshal Dillon."

"I simply cannot...." Vivian Strauss began, but a slight wave of the hand from Adams quickly silenced her.

"An offer?" Adams said, leaning forward in his chair.

McCabe's face began to relax to a more flesh-colored tone. "Yes, a position, within the Special Detective Unit. He would be a perfect fit for a position we've been desperately trying to fill."

"Well, I wonder if it wouldn't be prudent to check with your superiors before you made such an outrageous claim," Strauss said, raising an eyebrow and smiling coldly.

McCabe stared at her for a long moment, thinking, *Your career here in this country is finished,* while his face morphed back up from red to crimson. He took a deep breath, pulled a briefcase up from the floor, and laid it on the conference table.

"I can assure you, I'm nothing if not prudent," he said, giving a cold stare to Strauss. He took his time snapping the locks open on the briefcase. Dillon half-expected him to pull out the bottle of Midleton whiskey and glasses from the previous night, but McCabe simply removed a manila file folder and set it on the table.

He closed the briefcase, placed it back on the floor, then folded his hands neatly in front of him like the perfect student. "It would seem to me you have two options at this point. You can continue in the direction you've started, pillorying the Marshal. All well and good, at least until you're linked to the character assassination which..." he opened the file and pulled out some documents, "which will happen almost immediately after this meeting once the Irish Independent and the Irish Times publish this article, complete with hospital pictures." He handed a document over to Adams, four pages actually, neatly typed, double-spaced and stapled together in the upper left-hand corner.

"Of course, the RTE interview we've set up for this afternoon will get the word out sooner. All the papers across the country will no doubt pick up the story, not to mention the internet. Does the term 'viral' have any connotations to either of you?"

Adams picked up the document, read the first few lines, turned to the second page, read a line or two, paged through the final two pages then quickly decided the safest place to be was to get as far away from this situation as fast as possible.

"Under the circumstances, it will now most likely make sense for our government to request your recall, Miss Strauss," McCabe said. "And I can assure you, Mr Adams, that we have a variety of friends in all facets of the American government, starting at the top with your president. Now, that said, let me offer an alternative. You've an opportunity at some very good press, not that the United States would ever need any." He paused for a moment.

"Oh?" Adams said.

"Yes. It would seem a shame to throw it all away and kick little old Ireland to the curb in the process." McCabe flashed the slightest of smiles and waited.

Adams gave a barely perceptible nod, then raised an eyebrow.

Strauss's head seemed to develop a slight tremor, moving almost as if she'd taken a small taste of something very unpleasant. She pursed her lips, although no sound emerged.

Finally Adams broke the silence. "You're proposing that Marshal Dillon be assigned to your unit? Does this mean he would be residing here, in your country? In Ireland?"

"I've the visa and appropriate paperwork here," McCabe said, and handed a sheaf of papers held together with a large paperclip across the table to Adams. "It only requires the Marshal's signature for it to be processed before the week is out."

"And his compensation, Dillon's. An Garda Síochána will be responsible for that?"

"In accordance with our scales of renumeration."

"There'll be no fallout from the armed circumstance? Nothing regarding his carrying weapons in the capital? Nothing that would reflect badly on the Marshals Service?"

"Quite to the contrary. As I stated earlier, he saved the lives of two members of our force, both Irish citizens. He was wounded himself and managed to subdue three assailants. We view him as a hero."

Adams seemed to think about that for a moment, then turned to Strauss. "This would seem to answer our concerns. He's out of our hair and off the payroll. Not exactly the way we'd planned, but the end result is the same, perhaps even better for everyone."

"Well yes, except for the fact that he'll be here, in Ireland. I didn't bargain for...."

"It works," Adams said and glanced at his watch. "If I hurry I can catch a flight to Charles de Gaulle Airport and be back in New York this evening."

"But this isn't what we...."

"This is the best we're going to get, Vivian. I suggest you smile, agree, and you might still make it to London this evening." With that Adams stood, and extended his hand to McCabe. "It's been...interesting, Detective

Chief Inspector. Very interesting. Marshal, I wish you all success in your new career. If I might make a suggestion, get back to your hospital bed and give that shoulder a rest. It's been quite the experience for me, I must say. But apparently you're the hero, at least here. Good luck." He pulled out a business card from his suit coat and handed it to McCabe. "If you'll copy me with the paperwork, merely for our records, I would appreciate it, Detective Chief Inspector," he said, then turned and walked out of the room.

Vivian Strauss pulled a purse from the floor. The purse was brown leather, and large enough to hide a small child in. She slung it over her shoulder and said, "Apparently anything can be condoned as long as you've the proper people on your side." Then she headed toward the door.

"I wasn't joking. We will be filing a formal complaint requesting your immediate departure from the country. And a word to the wise, I wouldn't plan on returning anytime soon. Your name will be on a watch list by the close of the day. Good day," McCabe said.

She stormed out of the room, then halfway down the hall let out a loud scream.

"I don't think she'd be much fun this weekend, or any weekend for that matter," McCabe laughed, then faced Dillon. "Well done, you. Now, you've a week to make a full recovery, and then it's to work, we've lots to do. They'll be doing a follow-up exam this afternoon and hopefully discharging you. We'll

207

be back and get you settled into your apartment once you've been officially discharged."

"Apartment?"

"Well, you can't very well live here now, can you?"

"No, it's just that I hadn't planned on...."

"You leave the planning to us. Nurse Lin, if you'd be so kind as to take the good Marshal back to his room, please. Maybe remove that ridiculous bandage with the fake blood before someone with some brains spots it and starts asking questions."

"Thank you," Dillon called as Lin rolled him out the door.

"Maybe save the thanks until you see what we've got in store for you," McCabe laughed.

Chapter Thirty-Two

She paid the taxi then stepped out, took a deep breath and walked up the circular drive. She'd been past the place a half-dozen times over the last two years, but never in her life thought that she'd be invited to pay a visit. She climbed the front steps, took a deep breath and rang the doorbell. She quickly brushed her blonde hair back from the side of her face, cleared her throat and struck a pose. The honor of being called to Alexei Bazanov's home wasn't lost on her. The door eventually opened and a large man with a shaved head stood in the doorway, looking down at her.

Her thick blonde hair was curled in a sexy way and just barely brushed against her shoulders. Her body looked ripe for the taking, and he thought that under different circumstances he'd love to do unnatural things to her, use her for an hour or two, maybe a night, and then discard her. But the circumstances were what they were, and so he smiled and hoped he appeared kindly.

"Miss Fedorov?" he said in Russian.

"Yes." She smiled eagerly and nodded, thrilled that he knew her name. "Mr. Bazanov asked to see me," she said, hoping the statement might give her at least a small sense of authority.

"Yes, we've been expecting you. Please, please, come in. Your first time here, I believe. I hope you didn't have any trouble finding us."

"No, none whatsoever," she said, leaving out the part that everyone knew the mansion where Alexei Bazanov lived.

"He's been waiting for you in his office. This way please," he said, and led her down a massive hallway with elegant plaster cornices and ceiling roses at least two hundred years old. They passed two massive, mahogany wooden doors. Large oil paintings in heavy gold frames hung on the walls. Russian scenes, she guessed, trees without leaves, windswept landscapes, and snow. They reminded her of her childhood, the village that had offered her no future whatsoever.

She appraised the figure in front of her as they walked, groaned inwardly at the thought of him rolling over on top of her. One could only hope you'd be able to finish him quickly. He stopped and knocked softly on the door next to an uncomfortable-looking antique couch sitting just before the massive staircase.

"Mr. Bazanov is inside." He smiled, turned the ornate brass knob and opened the door for her, then pulled it closed once she stepped inside.

"Ahh, Miss Fedorov, thank you so much for gracing me with your presence," Alexei Bazanov said, springing out of the black leather chair behind his desk. The desk was a massive thing, carved, with inset panels of darker burled wood. The top of the desk was covered with tooled green leather trimmed in gold. A matching piece of green marble rested on the desktop with a gold clock inset in the center and two gold lions, one on either side of the clock.

Bazanov himself was surprisingly short, maybe just an inch taller than herself. From the pictures she'd seen, and his reputation, she'd always thought he'd be over six feet. His hair was trimmed very short on the sides, and long on top, combed straight back with a couple of strands hanging down along the side.

"Let me get you something, a vodka," he said.

A vodka? At just after ten in the morning? This must be the way the other half lives. "Yes, thank you," she finally said, hoping she'd hid her surprise.

"Please, please," he said, handing her a small cut crystal glass a moment later. "Let's take a seat over here on the couch." He pointed toward the couch using his hand holding the vodka bottle. Once they were seated he smiled. She smiled back, and then it was quiet for a very long moment. He filled the crystal glasses, raised his glass in a toast,

211

clinked against hers and said, "Tvoye zdorovye," then downed the vodka.

She did the same, coughed, turned her head and shuddered. It was good vodka, probably the most expensive she'd ever had, but downing the glass was something she'd never quite been able to do.

He quickly refilled her glass, flashed a nervous smile, refilled his own glass then looked at her for a moment. "Miss Fedorov, in my position I've been blessed to be able to help people in need. I've been able to provide my services to many people, and in return I've received their friendship and their loyalty."

She nodded, smiled and wondered where this was going.

"Your brother, Borya was such a man, a dear friend, and loyal. Very loyal."

Borya, her crazy little brother? What had he got to do with this?

"It is my sad duty to inform you that Borya was killed earlier this week. This past Sunday, actually."

"Borya? No, sorry, but I think you must be mistaken. I only spoke with him the other day. Borya," she said, raising her voice, hoping the mere act would make it so. "No, I'm sorry, but you must have the wrong one. He, he..." She was trying to think. *Was it Saturday or Sunday when she last spoke to him?* He bragged about something important he was going to do, something that would change everything. And she didn't have time to talk because she was late to meet girlfriends at Dicey's for a night of dancing and drink, and then she remembered, that had been Saturday night.

"Borya?"

"I'm afraid so."

"But how? What happened?" It wasn't making sense, and she held onto the thought that there must be some mistake.

"He was killed," Alexei said, pausing for a moment before he added, "By an American."

"Killed? But why? No, it can't be. What happened?"

"We're not sure yet. We're trying to learn more. When I know something you'll be the first one I tell. It's just that at this moment it's unclear exactly what happened."

"And, and this American? Has he been arrested? Do they know where he is?"

"He has not been arrested. When he is found, and we will find him, he will be killed."

She picked up her glass, looked at it for a brief moment, then downed the contents and barely flinched. "When you find him, I want to kill him."

"I don't know if that can be possible. He is some sort of police officer, and even now may be headed back to the United States. We're looking, but so far…." He held his hands out, indicating they were at a loss, at least for the moment.

"If loyalty is what you want, please promise me. I'll do anything, anything at all. But I want to kill him. I want to look in his eye, tell him my brother's name and then kill him. I want my brother's name, Borya Fedorov, to be the last thing the bastard ever hears."

The End

Thanks for taking the time to read <u>Welcome</u>. If you enjoyed reading the first work in the Jack Dillon Dublin Tales series, please feel free to leave a review on Amazon.

Books by Mike Faricy

The following titles are stand alone;

Baby Grand
Chow For Now
Slow, Slow, Quick, Quick
Merlot
Finders Keepers
End of the Line

Irish Dukes (Fight Card Series)
written under the pseudonym Jack Tunney

All stand alone titles
are available on Amazon.

*The following titles comprise
the Dev Haskell series;*

Russian Roulette: Case 1
Mr. Swirlee: Case 2
Bite Me: Case 3
Bombshell: Case 4
Tutti Frutti: Case 5
Last Shot: Case 6
Ting-A-Ling: Case 7
Crickett: Case 8
Bulldog: Case 9
Double Trouble: Case 10
Yellow Ribbon: Case 11
Dog Gone: Case 12
Scam Man: Case 13
Foiled: Case 14
What Happens in Vegas : Case 15
Art Hound: Case 16
The Office: Case 17

The following titles are Dev Haskell novellas;

Dollhouse
The Dance
Pixie
FORE!

Twinkle Toes
(a Dev Haskell short story)

The Dev Haskell series
is available on Amazon.

The following titles comprise the
Corridor Man series
written under the pseudonym
Nick James;

Corridor Man
Corridor Man 2: Opportunity knocks
Corridor Man 3: The Dungeon
Corridor Man 4: Dead End
Corridor Man 5: Finger
Corridor Man 6: Exit Strategy
Corridor Man 7: Trunk Music

Corridor Man novellas;
Corridor Man: Valentine
Corridor Man: Auditor
Corridor Man Howling

The Corridor Man series
is available on Amazon.

The following titles comprise the Jack Dillon Dublin Tales series written under the pseudonym Patrick Emmett;

Welcome
Jack Dillon Dublin Tale 1

Sweet Dreams
Jack Dillon Dublin Tale 2

Mirror Mirror
Jack Dillon Dublin Tale 3

Silver Bullet
Jack Dillon Dublin Tale 4

Fair City Blues
Jack Dillon Dublin Tales 5

The Jack Dillon Dublin Tales series
is available on Amazon.

Contact Mike;
Email:
mikefaricyauthor@gmail.com
Twitter: @Mikefaricybooks
Facebook:
DevHaskell or MikeFaricyBooks
Website:
http://www.mikefaricybooks.com

Thank you!

Made in the USA
Las Vegas, NV
14 January 2022

41441094R00125